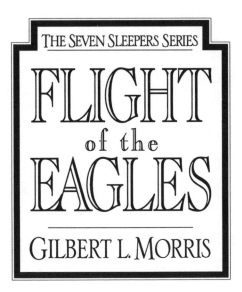

THE SEVEN SLEEPERS SERIES

FLIGHT
of the
EAGLES

GILBERT L. MORRIS

MOODY PRESS
CHICAGO

ISBN: 0-0824-3681-1

11 13 15 17 19 20 18 16 14 12

Printed in the United States of America

To my grandchildren,
Dixie, Andrea, Zachary, and Laura

Contents

Foreword

This is a story about a very ordinary boy named Josh Adams and a very strange adventure he had. Some of you may want to ask, "Is it a true story?" I can only say that a true story is not one that has happened but one that *could* happen. If you are the sort of person who finds "real" people, such as Zachary Taylor, more interesting than Robin Hood, you had better stop here and find a "true" history book.

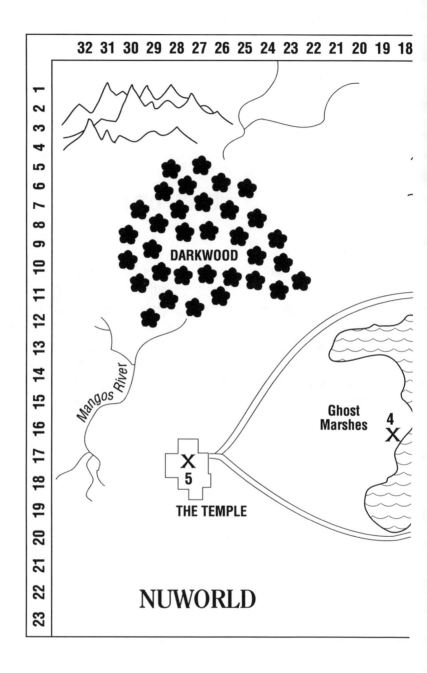

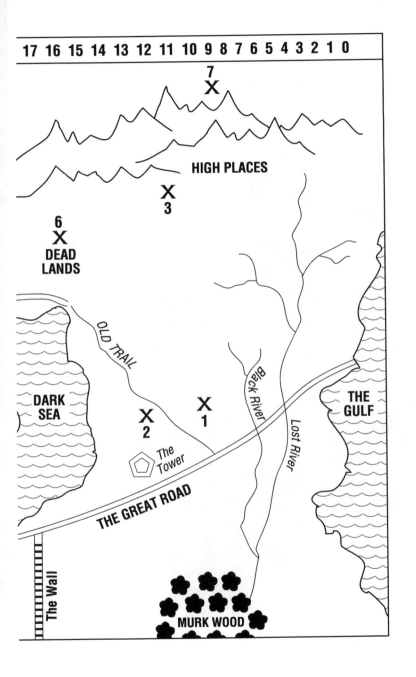

1

The Last Night on Earth

Josh Adams lived with his parents in a small brick house not far from a large city but close to the open country-side. For the first thirteen years of his life—up until about a year before the adventure began—he had led a happy life, enjoying his parents, his school, and his friends. But all at once he shot up until he was more than a head taller than any of his friends. He was, of course, quite clumsy, and several of his schoolmates made matters worse by calling him "Ichabod Crane" or just "Icky" for short.

His father noticed that Josh began to walk with a slouch that made him even more conspicuous. One day, he put his arm around Josh's thin shoulders and pointed at the collie puppy next door, all legs and falling over his own feet.

"That's you, Josh," Mr. Adams said.

"Yeah," Josh muttered grimly.

"And that's what you will be before too long."

Josh stared at the perfectly shaped grown-up collie, then shook his head sadly. "Not in a million years. I'm just a clumsy jerk!" he said.

It was not only that he was clumsy and towered over his friends, though that seemed bad enough. But just when he felt most isolated from what he bitterly called normal people, Sarah came to live at the Adamses' house.

Josh had heard his family talk about some old college friends whose daughter might come for a visit, but when he came home from school one afternoon to find her already moved in, he was caught off guard.

He opened the door and found his mother standing there with a very pretty girl a little younger than himself.

"Josh, this is Sarah Collingwood. We've told you about her so often. Sarah, this is Josh."

Now if Sarah had been a boy, or even if she had been tall and awkward, or if she had been plain, Josh would probably have taken the small hand she reached out to him, and he would have found a close friend, which he sorely needed. However, since Sarah was small, graceful, and quite pretty, Josh turned red and ignored the hand, muttering, "Hi ya," under his breath.

"You know, Josh, we told you that Sarah might get to make a visit, but her parents have agreed that she can stay for the rest of the school year."

Mrs. Adams hugged Sarah warmly. "It'll be so nice for me to have a girl in the house. Josh and his father hunt and fish together all the time—now you and I can do things together."

"I hope so, Mrs. Adams." Sarah smiled. She had large brown eyes and very black hair.

Josh sneaked a glance and saw that she was slender. Her hands were so small that they made his own look like catchers' mitts.

"Josh, I want to discuss some business with your father. Sarah and I have been so busy talking that we haven't even gotten her things up to her room. Why don't you help her do that, and I'll be back soon to start supper."

She gave Sarah another hug, then left them alone.

Josh looked everywhere but at Sarah. His thoughts were gloomy. He was thinking how Sarah would be just like the other girls at school who made fun of him and his appearance.

Now there were two things wrong with this. In the first place, the girls were not making fun of him. Instead, they were noticing that he was filling out and getting to be good-looking.

In the second place, Sarah did not disapprove of him. If Josh had had the courage to look at her, he would have seen a rather frightened young girl, uncertain at being in a strange place and very anxious to be liked by the young man before her. She had just passed out of the leggy, coltish stage that some girls go through and knew very well Josh's feelings of inadequacy.

"Josh," she said shyly, "I hope you don't mind my coming to live here."

Josh wanted to say that he was glad that she'd come, but he covered up his feeling by answering roughly, "Well, where are your folks? Why'd they send you here?"

Sarah said, "They're missionaries in Africa."

"Missionaries! Your folks are preachers?"

Actually, Josh enjoyed going to church with his parents. However, he was afraid of being considered "soft," so he affected the tough manner he had seen in others. "Well, don't go trying to preach at me!"

Sarah stiffened and said sharply, "Don't worry about that! I just wish I was home!"

"Why'd you come anyway?"

"My parents said it was because I needed a good school—but it wasn't really that." Her voice trembled slightly as she continued. "The real reason is that there's a revolution in Africa, and it's dangerous. I didn't want to come!"

Josh saw to his dismay that she was about to cry, and he *almost* did the right thing. He *almost* smiled, and he *almost* told Sarah it was great to have her. He *almost* assured her that they would be great friends and that her parents would be safe. And if he had done this, the following days would have been much more comfortable.

But Sarah was too pretty, and Josh was too afraid of girls.

He merely shrugged toughly. "I don't guess you have

13

to worry about your folks. Missionaries never get killed in revolutions."

Instantly Sarah drew back and blinked away the tears.

Josh could have bitten his tongue, but it was too late.

From that moment, Sarah kept as far from him as possible. They ate at the same table and even walked to school together. But there was a wall between them that Josh could not break down. Sarah found new friends at school, and Josh felt even more sorry for himself, forgetting that he had closed the door on her.

* * *

It was almost a year after Sarah came that the adventure began. Josh was sound asleep one winter evening when he heard his name being called.

"Josh! Josh! Wake up!"

He sat up at once, shielding his eyes against the overhead light. He saw his father standing over him, his face pale and tense.

"What's the matter, Dad?" he cried in sudden fear.

"Son," Mr. Adams said, "we've got to go to the silo. Get dressed quickly."

Josh's father was a scientist who did some sort of secret work for the government. The silo had been part of an old underground missile base that had been made into a laboratory.

"What's wrong, Dad?" Josh asked as he started pulling on his clothes. "Is something wrong with Mom?"

"No, I'll explain on the way, Josh. I've given Sarah a call, but you go by and make sure she's up. Meet us in the car." He rushed out of the room without another word.

Josh scrambled into his clothes, shaking from cold and fear. When he was dressed, he ran down the hall and knocked on Sarah's door.

She opened it at once. She was fully dressed too, and Josh saw that her eyes were large with fear.

"Hurry up," Josh said. "My mom and dad are waiting for us in the car."

"Do you know what's wrong?" Sarah whispered.

"No. Come on, let's hurry."

"I—I think I know what it is," she said. "I think something's wrong with my parents."

Josh paused for a moment. He knew there had been a lot of trouble in the African nation where Sarah's parents were doing their missionary work.

"Well," he said, "I don't think that's it. Why would we be going to the lab in the middle of the night for that?"

Quickly they scurried out of the house through the freezing cold and piled into the car where Josh's parents were waiting.

As soon as Josh slammed the door, Mr. Adams sent the car onto the highway so suddenly that the young people were thrown back against the rear of the seat. Josh had never known his father to drive like that before. Something had to be very wrong.

"Josh and Sarah," Mr. Adams said quietly, "you might have guessed what's happened."

"Is it something about my parents?" Sarah asked quickly.

"Well, Sarah, I just don't know about them, but we're *all* in danger now."

Suddenly Josh knew what was happening. "It's a war, isn't it, Dad?"

"Yes, Josh, it is. There's been an attack on the East Coast, and reports are that the rest of the country will be bombed at any time. We have to get to the silo."

Then he turned on the radio, and they heard the familiar voice of the president.

". . . indeed the most terrible crisis in the history of

mankind. I have declared a national emergency, and our armed forces are even now being deployed for our nation's defense. I must warn you, my fellow Americans, that not just our own country but the entire world stands on the brink of destruction tonight. I ask that you pray for—"

Squeak! Crash! Suddenly, the radio went dead. Mr. Adams could find no other station on the dial. The airways were quiet, and everyone in the car fell just as silent.

Soon they pulled up before the plain concrete building that contained the silo. They got out of the car just as the eastern sky was beginning to turn red.

"It's almost daylight," Josh said.

Mr. Adams paused and looked at the sky. Then he said quietly, "That's not the sun."

They moved quickly into the silo. Turning on the lights, Mr. Adams led the way down a winding staircase. As they descended into the earth, Josh had the feeling that he was being buried alive. He suspected that Sarah held the same thought.

Finally, they came to the foot of the stairs. After Mr. Adams unlocked a strange steel door, they entered the silo.

Josh had never been inside the silo. He had always thought it would be filled with huge banks of scientific equipment like the spaceships in movies. But all he saw was a small room and something that looked like a white coffin covered with clear plastic. Several tubes and cables were attached to a machine next to the wall. There was nothing else in the room except a small desk.

Josh and Sarah looked at the casketlike device.

"What's *that* for, Dad?" Josh asked with sudden fear.

"It's for you, Josh," Mr. Adams said quietly.

"But—what's it *for*?" Josh asked. He felt Sarah moving closer until she touched him, and he knew that she was sharing his alarm.

16

Mr. Adams put his arm around his wife and looked at the two youngsters, his face deadly serious. "The world is ending tonight—for a while, at least."

Josh felt Sarah's small hand creep into his. He took her hand and held it tight.

"This war won't be like any that you've ever read about," Mr. Adams said. "It will probably last only a day or two—but it will be so terrible that the world as we know it now will be gone forever."

Suddenly, there was a rumble like distant thunder. They all looked up. Josh knew that anything they could hear so far under the earth through heavy concrete had to be something monstrous. He felt the concrete vibrate under his feet. Then there was a buzzing sound, and a red light went on over the door.

Mr. and Mrs. Adams looked at one another. Then Mrs. Adams put her arm around Sarah and said, "Sarah, it's time for you to go."

"Go!" Sarah cried and held Josh's hand more tightly. "Go where? I—I want to stay with Josh."

"You can't, child," Mr. Adams said. "You see, this is what we've been working on ever since we saw that war was coming." He put his hand on the plastic canopy. "You can call it—well—call it a 'Sleep Capsule,' for that's its purpose. You'll just go to sleep. Then, when it's safe, you'll be awakened—safe and alive."

Josh's mother spoke gently to Sarah. "You see, there aren't two capsules in one place. This way, if something happens, some of the capsules will be sure to get through."

"No one knows where the capsules are," Mr. Adams said. "It's a closely guarded secret. But after you come out, there'll be a way to get all of you together—and start a better world!"

The buzzer sounded, and the red light flashed insistently.

17

"Come along, Sarah," Mrs. Adams said. "I insisted on going with you to your location so you wouldn't be alone."

She turned and held Josh in her arms tightly and said, "Good night, son. I love you very much."

Josh's mother turned suddenly and moved to the desk. Opening a drawer, she took out a leather-bound book. She stroked the covers, then said, "Josh, for many years I've kept a journal. In it I've put down all the things I believe in." She held it out to him, and there were tears in her eyes. "I want you to have it, son."

Josh took the book and held it carefully. He'd seen his mother writing in her journal and knew that she prized it highly. "I'll—I'll keep it, Mom. And I'll read it too."

Mrs. Adams suddenly threw her arms around him again, whispering, "Whatever happens, Josh, we'll meet again."

Then she released him, and Josh's father opened the massive steel door. An officer in uniform was standing outside. Josh's mother pulled Sarah through the door, and, just as it swung closed, Josh caught one glimpse of Sarah's pale face.

With a catch in her voice, Sarah said, "Josh, I—I'll see you soon!"

Then the door clanged shut. Josh was left alone with his father.

"Dad—what about you and Mom? Where will you be?"

"Well, son, it's very complicated. You'll just have to trust me. We don't have much time, and—" A heavy rumble shook the silo again. "It's time, son."

He must have seen the stark fear in the boy's eyes, and he asked gently, "Josh, do you remember last year when you and I climbed down the mountain in Colorado?"

Joshua nodded silently.

18

"Well, you remember how you were afraid to go down the face of the steepest cliff? You said, 'I'll go down if you'll hold the rope, Dad.'"

"I remember," Josh said.

"Well, I'm asking you to do that again. I know you're afraid—anyone would be—but if you'll trust me, *I'll hold the rope!*"

Joshua looked into his father's face for a long moment. Then he said slowly, "All right, Dad. I'll do it."

"Good!" Josh's father hugged him. Then he stepped back and said, "Josh, for the last few weeks, something has been happening to me. I've been having—well, *dreams* you might call them."

He stopped, and there was the strangest look on his face. "I'm a scientist, and I've always laughed at such things, but Josh, night after night, I've had the same dream."

"What was it, Dad?" Josh asked, seeing his father hesitate.

"Well, a man comes to me. I can never see his face, and I can't really remember what he says. But he always says the same thing, and I can't understand any of it."

"Are you afraid of him, Dad?" Josh questioned.

"No! I always feel better after one of these—visits. It's like everything's going to be all right. But I just can't remember *him* much—only the song."

"The song?" Josh asked.

"Yes. You know I don't sing very well. But almost every night for a long time, he's been teaching me a song. I don't understand it much, but I think it has something to do with you and Sarah, and what you'll find when you go up to the world again."

"What does the song say?"

"I made a tape of it—the tape is in there," Mr. Adams said, pointing to a brown case. "And some other things. I wanted to study the song, but it must be for you and Sarah. I'm almost sure the man in my dream told me that. You can keep your mother's journal in the case too."

The lights dimmed again, and Josh's father motioned for his son to climb into the white box.

After Josh was comfortably settled, his father moved to unhook the props of the plastic canopy. Then he stopped and nodded to the control board.

"See that switch, son?"

Josh saw one red switch marked simply AWAKE.

"One day, someone will throw that switch. Then you and Sarah and some others will come out of places like this and go into the world. I don't know what kind of a place that world will be—but it won't be like anything you've ever known. Now it's time for us to go, and I want you to promise me to do two things—OK, son?"

"Yes, Dad."

"First, when you come out of here, I want you to believe the song—the one on the tape. Then, for your mother, obey the book—the one she's given you. Will you say those things over and over again, Josh?"

Josh began to say the words. "Believe the song, obey the book."

As he repeated them, he heard his father say quietly, "Good night, Josh. I'll be near you."

Then the lid closed, and there was a sound of escaping gas. Josh began to dive down into a deep sleep.

He found himself saying again, "Believe the song . . . obey the book . . ." just as he dropped off into a strange sleep. He heard himself murmur, "Good night, Dad. I'll see you . . ."

Then he became part of the darkness that was all about.

2

The First Sleeper

Someone far off was calling his name over and over, but Josh tried to close his ears and slip back into the comfortable cocoon of warm darkness.

"Joshua—awake!" the faint voice insisted. *"Awake, Joshua, awake!"*

As he slowly came to full consciousness, Josh thought at first that one of his parents was calling him for breakfast. He slowly opened his eyes, expecting to see his familiar bedroom.

Instead, there was nothing but white overhead. At the same time, he realized that he could hear none of the familiar wake-up noises—kitchen sounds, someone in the shower singing, early morning traffic—none of these. All he heard was a quiet hiss, like a huge tire leaking air.

Josh turned his head and looked around wildly. There was only one very small light in the room, but when he saw the bare walls and remembered suddenly his last moment awake, his mouth went dry with fear.

He began to shout, "Dad! Mom!" He tried to sit up, but his forehead struck the clear plastic shell that covered the bed. "Ow," he cried, and then, before he could utter another sound, the plastic cover swung back, and he was free.

Quickly he scrambled off the bed and peered into the semidarkness. He saw nothing and cried out more loudly than before.

"Dad! Mom!"

But not even an echo stirred in the darkness.

Where's the door? His thoughts were in a swirl. He had to get out of here!

He moved to the wall, groping until he found the single door into the room. He fumbled for the knob. There was no knob, no handle . . . nothing.

Panic grabbed him, and he began to beat on the door with his fists.

"Someone let me out! Please! Let me out! Please, let me out!"

He never remembered afterward how long this went on, but when he finally slumped down on the floor, his voice was worn thin and his fists hurt.

Then Josh recalled a story he had read about a man who had been walled up, buried alive. Buried alive! He huddled in the dim light, his mind racing to seek some answer, but nothing came. Then, just as he was about to begin crying out again, the hissing noise stopped. The room was totally silent. Silent, that is, except for—

Except for what? He held his breath, and then he heard it—a faint, raspy wheezing.

Now Josh, who had been desperately crying for someone to come, was terrified at the knowledge that someone was with him! He scrunched himself into the smallest possible shape, peering blindly into the dark corners. Again he heard the steady wheeze of someone's breath.

Moments passed. He had almost decided that the noise was some sort of machinery or perhaps the wind, when out of the darkness a voice said, "Don't be afraid, young man."

It was a high, scratchy voice, to which Josh managed to whisper a question. "Who are you?"

"My name, you mean?" the scratchy voice asked. "Well, I haven't used a name in so long I've almost forgotten. But you can call me—Crusoe." The voice laughed softly. "I guess I've been marooned long enough to have that name."

Josh got to his feet and asked, "Isn't there more light? I can't see you."

"Well, there is, but I didn't turn it on before because—well, you might have been a little frightened at the sight of me. But here we are."

There was a quiet click, and the room suddenly grew bright. Josh gazed fearfully at the small figure across the room. He had been expecting something terrible—a gorilla-like form or something like Frankenstein's monster. What he saw was *different*, but certainly not frightening.

Crusoe, as he called himself, reminded Josh of a very old kangaroo, perhaps because of the way he hopped across the room, holding his hands together in front of him.

His face *was* a little frightening—wrinkled like a dried prune, with several white scar patches across his cheeks. He had a pointed nose and big front teeth that stuck out. But the brown eyes peering from the scarred and wrinkled face were warm and friendly.

Crusoe was bent over almost like a hunchback, and he had to twist his head to look up at the taller Josh. Softly he asked, "Are you hungry?"

All of a sudden Josh realized that he *was* hungry, hungrier than he could ever remember. But questions overwhelmed him. He hurriedly began to ask, "What's happened? Where is everyone? And what—"

"Later! Later!" Crusoe wheezed. "First, eat! Then we can talk. Come, come!"

Crusoe pulled Josh toward the door, then stopped and said something in a language Josh did not understand. The door swung smoothly open. In his queer hopping gait, Crusoe pulled and pushed Josh down the hall into a room that looked and smelled like a kitchen.

23

"Sit here, Joshua," Crusoe said, pushing him into a chair.

Josh noticed that the old man knew his name, but before he could ask how, he found hot food in front of him. It smelled delicious, though he didn't recognize any of it.

"What is it?" he asked between bites.

"It's *good*! That's what it is," Crusoe said. "Just eat, and don't ask questions."

Crusoe kept hopping off his high stool to refill Josh's plate with food and his own cup with some sort of red drink.

Finally, Josh could not eat another bite. "It was very good, Mr. Crusoe. Now can I ask some questions?"

"Yes." Crusoe nodded. "However, you may not like my answers."

Josh asked the first question that flew into his mind. "Where are my mother and father?"

Even as he spoke, he saw something in Crusoe's eyes that made his heart turn cold.

Crusoe looked steadily at Josh for a long moment, then spoke gently, "You must begin to be brave, Joshua."

He put one thin hand, almost like a tiny claw, on Josh's arm and said, "They're gone, my boy."

A wave of pain and fear engulfed Josh. Tears welled into his eyes, but he held them back as he saw Crusoe watching him, nodding his head in sympathy. He swallowed hard, trying to choke back the sobs.

"Later, Joshua—" Crusoe nodded again "—later, you will mourn your parents as you should. For now, don't be ashamed of honest tears," he added, as Josh tried to blink them away. "I think you can see much farther through a tear than you can through a telescope."

Josh managed a small smile. Then he asked, "How did it happen?"

Hopping off his stool, Crusoe pulled out a large map. The terrain on the map seemed unfamiliar to Josh, though part of it, he thought, did look a little like something he had seen somewhere else.

"What place is that?" he asked.

"This is the world," Crusoe said, "as it is *now*—Nuworld is its name."

"But—it's all *different!*" Josh protested. "What happened?"

"There was a war, and terrible weapons were used," Crusoe said. "It wasn't like other wars. The bombs melted the ice caps and flooded whole nations. Florida and California both disappeared. And the bombs set off earthquakes, pushing up mountains. There are deserts now where there were once fertile fields. Your world is gone, Joshua."

"But it can't be," Josh protested. "It's only been a little while—" He paused, seeing Crusoe shake his head sadly. "How long has it been?" he asked slowly. He was somehow hoping that it had not been too long, no more than a few months or even a year or two. Perhaps he hoped that, if it had not been too long, he might find someone he had known.

"You have been asleep for fifty years, Joshua."

Josh felt as if he had been hit in the stomach. *"Fifty years!"* he whispered. "They're all dead then! Everyone I knew."

Crusoe reached up and took a small brown bottle from a cabinet. Then he poured some clear liquid into a glass and handed it to Joshua, saying. "Drink this."

Josh swallowed it obediently. The liquid burned his throat like fire, but it also drove away his faintness. "I'm all right now."

"Good boy, Joshua." Crusoe capped the bottle and put it back in the cabinet. "Now, perhaps we'd better—" Here he was interrupted as the door swung open and two dwarfs walked in.

At least they looked like dwarfs, those in the books that Josh had always loved. They were short, not much more than three feet tall, and fat as sausages. Their bellies gave promise of exploding any minute were it not for their broad black leather belts with shiny brass buckles. Both had fat red cheeks with small black eyes peering out from under impossibly bushy eyebrows. Both also had beards that came down almost to their belt buckles. The pair stared at Josh, mouths open, and he stared back at them, speechless.

"Joshua, this is Mat, and this is Tam," Crusoe said.

"Why, you're twins!" Josh said. "How can I tell you apart?"

The dwarf on the left sniffed and said, "That won't be hard. Just listen, and the one who talks a lot of happy nonsense without a grain of common sense—that one'll be him, Tam." With a thick forefinger, he prodded his brother, who was smiling broadly.

"Greetings!" the other dwarf said. "And if you hear anyone talking about doom and funerals and calamities —why, it'll be him, brother Mat."

Crusoe interrupted to say, "That's often the case with two like those. They're Gemini twins, Joshua."

"What's that?"

"After the Terror—the war, I mean—many sets of twins were born—"

"And many worse things!" Mat grumped.

"—and for some reason, many of these twins, though they looked exactly alike, were just the opposite in every other way. If one was rather happy, the other would be sure to be sad. If one was timid, the other would be a fighter—"

Mat interrupted. "And if one was foolish and always looked for pie-in-the-sky—" he poked Tam again "—the other would have to have enough caution and common sense for *two*."

"Ho!" Tam grinned. "And if one of them—" here he glanced slyly at his brother "—was sour and gloomy enough to curdle milk, why the other would have to have enough fun for *both*!"

"Don't get them started." Crusoe groaned. "They never agree on anything, and they can never in this world get away from one another."

"Why not?" Josh asked in surprise.

"Because there's something in them—nobody knows what it is—that makes it necessary for them to stay close. You never see *one* Gemini. If they get separated, the farther apart they get the weaker they become. And if they get too far apart, they both just die."

"Yep," Tam agreed cheerfully. "And when one goes —the other goes. *Pop*—off the other pops too! Dead as a bucket."

"If it *weren't* so," Mat muttered under his breath, "I'd have knocked this cheerful idiot in the head years ago!"

"You'll learn to trust them soon enough," Crusoe said. "They fight all the time, but they are always truthful. They also know a lot more than it appears they might."

At that moment, the brothers began to quarrel and seemed nearly ready to attack each other. But Crusoe got between them, trying to calm them down.

As Josh looked at the two dwarfs and the hunchbacked form of Crusoe, a lump rose again in his throat.

"What's wrong, Joshua?" Crusoe asked.

"I feel so—so *foreign*!" Josh said. "My whole world is gone, and all I see is dwarfs and—" He paused abruptly, for he had been about to say something about hunchbacked kangaroos. "Well, I just wish I could see some—normal people!"

"*Normal* people!" Mat suddenly roared. "Normal people, indeed! I like that! Haven't you told him yet, Crusoe?"

"Told me what?" Josh asked anxiously.

"Why, *we're* normal," Mat said loudly, pointing at Tam and himself. "You're the freak around here!"

"Now, Mat, that's no way to talk," Tam said.

"It's the truth, and that's what he needs to know. You can't feed him on sugar candy forever," Mat said grimly.

"What does he mean?" Josh asked Crusoe.

"Well, most of the 'normal' people like yourself were killed during the Terror. And those that were born afterward were different—like the Gemini twins."

"And a lot better off we are too," Tam cried. "Why, in the old days almost everybody looked pretty much alike. Now you got lots of variety!"

"Ho!" Mat sneered at his brother. "We've got variety all right! Giants to stomp you, Wolfpeople to tear your throat out, those nice Serpent-folk from the north to sink their fangs into you—"

He would have gone on, but Crusoe broke in. "Now, now, that's enough, Mat! It's true that strange effects resulted from the Terror, but you can find people to love and trust here, just as in Oldtime."

Even as Crusoe was talking, something was happening to Josh. In the din of the argument, a peculiar quiet had fallen on him, as if he were somehow surrounded and shut off from the outside world. And this quiet brought a peace that rushed into his troubled mind, blocking off all his fears.

Out of the silence came a faint voice, both familiar and loving. The voice was singing a song with words that he had never heard. Yet he knew that the words were true. And he began singing them softly as they came to him out of the silence.

28

"Some sleep beneath the heavy earth,
Some higher than the sky,
All waiting for a timely birth,
The Seven Sleepers lie.

"The house of Goél will be filled,
The earth itself will quake!
The beast will be forever stilled,
When Seven Sleepers wake!"

Josh finished the song and was startled at himself. It was as if he had heard another voice and not his own.

Crusoe, he saw, was smiling.

But suddenly Mat threw his soft cap on the floor and stomped it angrily. "Just what we need!" he snarled. "A *fanatic* to play keeper to. You don't believe that crazy nonsense?" he asked Josh.

"What do you mean?" Josh asked in confusion.

The dwarf sniffed. "Don't give me that."

"Wait a minute, brother," Tam interrupted. "Maybe there is something to the stories."

"There's something to it, all right—foolish superstition!" Mat stomped his cap again. "No one with any sense believes any of that ancient drivel."

"I don't understand," Josh protested.

"That old hunk of hokum about Seven Sleepers—that's what I mean."

Crusoe came and stood close to Josh. "Be quiet, Mat. You must remember that Joshua is somewhat like a baby. He doesn't know anything about the Promise."

"What promise?" Josh asked.

"Why, *the* Promise!" Tam cried. "The promise that one day there'll be an end to all the evil in the world—and things will be *good* again like they never were, and—"

"And that's the kind of talk that will get us all put in the Tower!" Mat grunted.

"But think of the old stories and the old songs all telling about the Seven Sleepers. What about all that?" Tam asked.

"Moonshine and applesauce," Mat snapped. "Who in his right mind believes all that garbage?"

"I do!" Tam answered cheerfully.

"Well, I don't," Mat returned.

They appeared ready for another violent disagreement, but Josh asked suddenly, "Mat, what about *me*?"

"Well," Mat asked suspiciously, "what about you?"

"He means," Crusoe said wheezily, "how can you explain his being here? We've all known that he's been asleep—all your lives you've known that. Now he's awake—just as I told you he would be one day."

"That's right!" Tam shouted excitedly. "Remember, brother, Crusoe always said the Sleeper would awake. You always said it could never be. Now there he is!" And in his excitement, Tam turned a cartwheel.

"Be still, you fool!" Mat looked hard at Joshua as if weighing him in his mind. Then he said, "Seven, eh? Well, where are they—the other six? You don't know. How will you find them? You don't know. What will you do after you find them? Don't know, do you?" He glared triumphantly at Tam, then pounded the map with his stubby fist. "Show me the places on the map!" he demanded.

Crusoe held up his hand for silence. "True places are never shown on a map. Joshua, do *you* believe the song you just sang? Because if you do believe, you have to do something about it, don't you? And if you don't believe, you can never make anyone else believe."

Once again the strange stillness fell over Josh, and he thought he heard a voice say, *"I'll be near you."* Then he looked at the misshapen figures before him. They reminded him of creatures from a nightmare.

30

Almost to himself Josh said, "Maybe this is all a dream. But I didn't dream the song. I don't even know what most of it means. But somewhere I think there are six other people just like me. And I'm either going to find them and wake them up—or else die trying."

"Hooray!" shouted Tam and turned another cartwheel.

"Humbug!" snorted Mat and stomped his cap.

Crusoe touched Josh's arm and whispered so low that Josh alone could hear him. "I'll help you, Joshua."

3
The Squire

Josh did little for the next two days but eat and sleep. During the hours he was awake, he listened over and over again to the tape that his father had left for him in the brown case.

There were seven songs in all, but Josh could make little sense out of any of them. The sound of his father's voice on the tapes affected him strangely. Sometimes he felt sad and lonely when he heard the voice, but other times he felt comforted, almost as if his father were still with him.

Josh also read much from his mother's journal, and there, too, he was comforted. The journal was well-worn, underlined on every page and with many notes written in his mother's hand.

Something else Josh found in the brown case was a map. It showed very few details, but there were some numbers running along the top and the sides.

On the third morning, he was studying the map when Mat walked by on an errand, carrying some food. "Mat, what are these numbers?" Josh asked.

"Let me see." Mat put his sack down and looked at the map. "This is an Oldtime map. Things aren't this way anymore."

"But what are the numbers?"

"Latitude and longitude, I suppose," Mat said. "Where did this map come from?"

"My father gave it to me." This seemed to be true enough to Josh.

Mat glanced at him shrewdly. "Do you think it's a map showing where the other Sleepers are?"

It was exactly what Josh had hoped, but he refused to admit it to Mat, who made fun of anything about the Sleepers. "I just wondered what the numbers meant," he lamely answered.

"It's so out of date now that it wouldn't do any good anyway," Mat said. He picked up his sack and left.

But Josh stared at the map for a long while. Then he played the tape for the twentieth time.

This time, it was Tam who passed by. He stopped to listen to the song.

"That's my father," Josh said, playing the second song on the tape:

> *"Far from ocean tides—*
> *Yet the sleeper lies*

> *"Where even sunlight seems to fail*
> *In the belly of the whale."*

"I don't have any idea what it means," Josh confessed.

Tam looked around. "Don't tell my brother," he whispered, "but I like poetry. I would like to hear all of these songs, if you don't mind."

Josh lowered his own voice, glad to share a secret with someone. "Here, Tam. I've copied them all out on this paper. Take them with you. If you think they mean anything, I wish you'd let me know."

"Well, I'm not much good at figuring poems out," Tam confessed. "I sure do like to read them though. They sound so nice."

All morning Josh thought about the problem of how to find the Sleepers, but his mind was a blank. About noon, he set out to find Crusoe and ask him more questions. He

34

searched all the rooms, but there was no one in the silo—
not even Mat and Tam.

Josh thought they might be outside, so he found his
way to the stairs and climbed to the outer entrance. The
door was fastened on the inside with a strong bar, but he
was able to lift it and push the door ajar. Evidently, the
door had not been touched for years, for it squealed loudly
as Josh swung it open.

My first sight of Nuworld, he thought nervously as he
stepped outside. It was not as shocking as he had feared.
Nothing was familiar, but he had expected that. There
were a few trees, stunted and misshapen to be sure, and a
line of rocks breaking through the earth.

Josh left the building and walked toward the spot
where the road had been. He quickly discovered that the
highway was no longer there. In every direction, he could
see only arid land broken by a few trees and outcroppings
of rock.

Josh continued to walk carefully to where the road
had been, but for some reason he did not call out for Crusoe or for the Gemini. There was an ominous stillness,
and he remembered what Mat had said about different
(and dangerous) people. He had gone less than three hundred feet and had just turned to go back to the silo when it
happened.

Out of the corner of his eye, he caught a glimpse of
movement to his right. Quickly he wheeled to face his
stalker. Then he froze, his mouth open. Fear so gripped
him that he could not speak.

Not ten feet away, coming from behind a large rock
straight at him, was a *giant!* It was a huge being, at least
ten feet tall. Its face, Josh saw in horror, was blunt and
stupid looking. It seemed the cruelest face he had ever
seen. There was a loud *thump thump thump* as the giant's
feet struck the earth.

Josh turned to run, but before he had taken two steps, an enormous hand closed around his arm. Then another enclosed his chest. He felt himself lifted into the air and drawn close to the evil-smelling creature. Desperately he cried for help.

"Help! Help, somebody! Help!" Then his entire face was swallowed by a monstrous hand, and he could neither call nor see.

Smothered inside the huge hand, Josh could feel the movements of the giant's lurching run. Then the giant seemed to stoop down for a moment, rise again, and stop. Through a crack between the creature's fingers, Josh peered out. They were in a bleak cave!

Josh could hear his own heart beating as he struggled to escape. He had read about cave trolls and other monsters, but his knowledge did him no service, for he felt totally hopeless.

Then suddenly the hand was removed and Josh heard —Crusoe's voice!

"Josh! What are you doing here?"

The giant lowered him to the floor.

Josh quickly pulled himself away and ran to Crusoe.

"Crusoe," he cried out. "There's a giant!"

Then Crusoe laughed, and Josh felt himself becoming angry. Was the old man deaf? Was he blind? Didn't he see the monster standing right there?

Josh glanced at the giant. The giant was laughing too—at least that was what it looked like. His thick features were squinted into what seemed to be a smile, and the big mountain of shoulders shook.

"What is this?" Josh asked Crusoe furiously. "If it's a joke, it's not very funny."

"No—" Crusoe laughed hoarsely "—I'm sorry, but why did you leave the shelter? Didn't you know it was dangerous?"

Josh stood there, feeling foolish. The giant, although of a monstrous size and bulging with muscles, did not look very fierce. Though his body resembled a slab from the Grand Canyon, his face was more like that of a huge toy bear.

"I hope I didn't hurt you," the big man apologized. "My name is Volka." He stuck out his hand.

"I was just startled at first," Josh said. "I'm Josh." He put out his hand to shake the massive paw Volka had pushed toward him. Josh's hand was lost in the vast palm, but the giant's shake was light as a feather.

"You shouldn't have gone outside alone, Joshua," Crusoe said seriously. "It's very dangerous."

"Yes," Volka said. "You nearly met a priest. One from the Sanhedrin was coming right toward you."

"A priest?" Josh said in surprise. "Why, that wouldn't be dangerous."

"This isn't your world, Joshua," Crusoe said sternly. "And now I think it's time for your education to begin."

"I'm going to school?" Josh asked in surprise and distaste.

"In a way." Crusoe led them back toward the silo. "By the way, never use the front door again. We keep it locked at all times. I'll show you the entrance we always use."

Crusoe led them into the silo and called to the Gemini to join them. Volka managed to squeeze through the door with a careful side step. Crusoe took them all into what seemed to be an old classroom. Then he spoke.

"We have some decisions to make."

They were all looking at Josh strangely, and he wondered what he had done.

"Has he decided?" Mat asked, waving a stubby hand toward Josh. "Because if he has, I want to go on record right now as being against it."

37

"You're always against everything," Tam said. "But I'm for it."

"Be quiet, you two," Crusoe commanded. "Joshua doesn't know what you're talking about."

Then he ignored the others and looked at the boy so intently that Joshua found it hard to meet his gaze.

"Joshua, you must decide."

"Decide what?"

"For years, I have heard of the Seven Sleepers. Now one of you has awakened. And you have heard a word of some kind that tells you that you must awaken the others. The Quest rests with you."

Josh felt small and helpless under Crusoe's gaze. "But I can't do anything. I couldn't even make the football team."

"I think the choice is clear. I think you've been— chosen to do this."

"Chosen by whom?" Josh asked in surprise.

"I don't know—yet." Crusoe paused and seemed to be listening to a voice far off.

Then he returned his attention to Josh and smiled. "I can only offer you this small consolation. If you decide to go, I'll go with you."

"And I'll go too!" Tam cried. He would have turned a cartwheel, but his brother held him back.

"I'll go if you want me to," Volka said.

Everyone looked at Mat, as though expecting him to object. To Josh's surprise he said, "I'll go too." He smiled sourly and added, "I'll have to if meathead Tam goes along, won't I?"

"What will it be, Joshua?" Crusoe asked.

Again the strange quiet surrounded Josh. He heard that faint echo of a voice whispering, *"I'll be near you."*

Josh said, "I'll go—but how will we find the way?"

They looked silently at one another.

Then Crusoe said firmly, "When the time comes, we'll be directed. But until then, you've got a lot to learn, Joshua."

"Well, that's the truth," Mat grumbled. "He doesn't even know the dialect."

Josh said in surprise, "Doesn't everyone speak English?"

"No," Crusoe replied. "The land has been so divided, and communications are so bad, that many different dialects have sprung up. But the common language is based on English, so it won't be too hard to learn."

"And you'll have to learn to take care of yourself," Volka said. "It's dangerous out there."

"Oh, I know how to shoot a rifle," Josh said eagerly.

They all laughed, and Tam reached behind a counter. He pulled out a long bow and a sheaf of feathered arrows tipped with hunting points. "Can you hit anything with this?" he asked.

"But why not a rifle?" Josh asked.

"Because there are none," Crusoe answered. "After the Terror, most modern weapons were destroyed. The new rulers made it illegal to have any modern weapons or to make any. I think they believe that rebellions are less likely if weapons are crude. So you'll have to learn to use a bow—and this."

Crusoe walked to a cabinet and opened it. He drew out a beautifully balanced sword. "Mat will be your teacher. He may well be the best swordsman in Nuworld."

Josh's heart sank at the gleam that suddenly appeared in Mat's dark eyes.

"How many *other* things do I have to learn?"

"Oh, not much," Tam said cheerfully. "How to ride a horse and take care of one, how to hunt, dress game, hitch a team, drive a wagon, how to pack an animal—"

"—read a map" —Crusoe took up the list— "as well as learn history, social customs—"

"—woodsmanship—," Volka added, "and how to use a knife and a staff, how to stalk—"

"And, of course, how to act a part," Crusoe said.

"Act!" Josh exclaimed in dismay. He had hated even the minor parts that he had played in school dramas. "Why do I have to be an actor?"

Crusoe grew deadly serious. His small hand tapped Josh's arm insistently.

"Because the Sanhedrin must *never* know who you are! You will have to pretend at all times to be something other than what you are. You can be a student or a half-wit or anything *except* one of the Sleepers!"

"What are the Sanhedrin?" Joshua asked.

"The courts, the army, the law—you name it, and they are behind it," Crusoe replied. A hard light appeared in his small bright eyes, and his lips tightened in anger. "And they know, so we hear, that the time is near for the Uprising, a move to unseat them and bring their evil ways to an end."

"It will be the rope or worse for us if they catch us!" Mat growled. He glared at Josh and added, "Better think twice about this, youngster. It's not a game."

Josh looked at the strange group, but their very strangeness was beginning to grow familiar to him. He answered simply, "Well, when do we start?"

Crusoe's face broke into a twisted grin.

"Right now," he said triumphantly.

* * *

The next month was torture for Josh.

Mat made the fencing lessons hellish. The lessons were so tough that Josh went to sleep dreading the next session. The sour-faced dwarf was a terror, driving the

40

boy from one end of the large room to the other. He would scream, then easily slip past Josh's clumsy guard and slap him cruelly with the flat blade.

"Get that guard up!" *Slap!*

"I thought you were anxious to learn!" *Slap!*

"Pick up your clumsy feet!" *Slap! Slap! Slap!*

During these sessions, Josh learned one lesson he would later treasure—to fight back with fiery determination, no matter how great the pain.

When Josh could hardly lift his sword arm, Tam would take him to a grove for archery practice. Many times Josh's fingers bled until the string was red, but he never complained. He began to be rewarded with the satisfying *thump* that sounded each time an arrow split the center of the target.

Volka used up whatever was left of Josh's strength, teaching him to saddle and unsaddle his horse. Josh's horse was a rather ugly roan pony named Roland. At first, Josh hated the horse because he had trouble staying on the spirited animal. But soon he came to love and trust the sturdy little beast.

One night, long after the others had gone to bed, Josh sat sleepily listening to Crusoe ramble on about the customs in Nuworld. Josh's mind was on his life as it now was. Suddenly he had a thought that sat him bolt upright.

"Say! Do you know what I am?" Then he laughed at Crusoe's blank look. "I mean—think of all I'm doing right now—fencing, shooting the bow, riding, hunting. Why, I'm a *squire*!"

Crusoe nodded seriously. "I think it's good for you to see yourself like that."

Josh smiled shyly, then shared his deepest secret with the old man. "I always loved stories about knights. But I never expected to be one."

"You're not one *yet*," Crusoe declared emphatically.

"And there's more to being a knight than slaying dragons!"

"What do you mean?"

"Knights did a lot of things, but they really had only one purpose. That was to destroy evil and find good. That sounds trite, I know, but Josh, that's the Quest—the search for goodness that all true knights pursued. And that's what you must pursue."

Josh looked down at his skinny frame with a shrug. "I don't look much like a knight," he said sadly.

"That doesn't matter," Crusoe snapped almost angrily. "What is important is that you think like one and act like one." Abruptly he got up and stalked away, leaving Josh to his own thoughts.

Perhaps it was this talk that led Josh to new heights of concentration. In any case, the next day during the fencing match he surprised Mat by driving straight at him so furiously that the dwarf lost his sword.

For one moment, the dwarf felt the point of Josh's sword against his throat, and Mat fell speechless.

Then Josh lowered his point and said quietly, "It's time to begin."

Stung by Josh's victory, Mat cried out loudly, "Just because you had a little luck—"

"I know, Mat, I know—but we *can't* wait forever! I'll never be as good at everything as all of you are. I say it's time."

"I think you're right." Josh turned and saw Crusoe standing in the doorway. "We'll meet tonight in the council room and decide what to do." He left as abruptly as he had appeared.

It was late that night by the time the work was done. For a while they sat silently in the flickering candlelight. When anyone spoke, it was usually to debate the next step in the plan.

"We can't just charge all over the country looking under rocks for the Sleepers," Mat almost shouted.

"Well, who said we would?" Tam grinned. "We'll simply keep our eyes and ears open. With the good luck that's due to us, we'll find them."

"Takes more than luck," said Volka slowly. "What do we have, really—to follow, I mean?"

Josh let the silence run on. Then he said with some hesitation, "Well, we have the songs. I don't understand them though."

"I found one thing in them," Tam said suddenly. "There's a certain combination of numbers in each one of them."

"What's that?" Crusoe said sharply.

"Look at them," Tam urged. "They're all in two parts, like this first one.

> *'Full deep the silent sleeper lies.*
>
> *'Down below the burning heath,*
> *deep within the empty sheath.'*

"You see, there are 8 syllables in the first line and 14 in the last line."

"But what does it mean?" Josh asked.

"I don't know," Tam admitted, "but every verse has something like it. See, the rest of them go like this—" he read off the list slowly "—10–15, 10–7, 18–15, 25–17, 16–8, 2–8."

"It might be a code, a secret message," Josh whispered excitedly.

They spent the next three hours trying to juggle the numbers around into something that made sense before finally giving up in despair.

Strangely, it was Mat who figured out the code, even though he had taken a sneering view of the whole affair. They were sitting in silence almost ready to go to bed, when suddenly Mat sat up straight and said, "I've got it!"

He jumped up and grinned so broadly that his sour face almost shattered. "I've got it," he hollered again and again. "I've got it!" Then he stopped. He forced his habitual scowl back on his face and added grumpily, "And it'll probably get us all killed."

"What is it, Mat?" they cried together.

"Do you have that map you were looking at the other day?" Mat asked Josh.

Josh took the map from his pocket and handed it over.

The dwarf spread it out on the table. "See these numbers along the top? And then these that run down the side? Well, I think they are the key to the songs."

"But how does it work?" Josh asked.

"The first number is 8–14. We find the 8 here on the top line," Tam said, moving his stubby finger across the paper, "then we find 14 on the side and where they cross—"

"Is where we are!" Crusoe interrupted in his cracked voice. He seized the paper and waved it around, stopping to show the others. "See, it's our exact location! Oh, things have changed, but I know the old land well, and 8–14 is the exact spot we are standing on."

Then he stopped, and a strange light came into his eyes. "Now I understand the song!" he said slowly, putting down the map. He lowered his reedy voice to only a whisper, *"'Down below the burning heath.'"* That's the land up there, and that's how my face got burned as it is, during the Terror.

"And that line *'Deep within the empty sheath.'* Why I didn't see it before, I don't know. This silo is a sheath of a kind. Instead of a sword, this sheath contained a missile.

But since the missile has been fired, the sheath is now *empty*. And here the Sleeper lies." He touched Josh's arm gently.

Josh said quickly, "You mean that the numbers from the song and the numbers on the map will tell us exactly where the Sleepers are?"

"Yes, I think so."

"Whee!" Tam shouted and turned a pair of cartwheels. "Why, we'll have them all awake in a week!"

"Not likely." Mat grunted. "Look where the next Sleeper is located." He had been looking at the two papers, and now his stubby finger came to rest at a place on the map.

They all looked at the spot.

Josh heard Crusoe draw a sharp breath. Looking around, he saw a tense expression on every face. "What's the matter?" Josh asked. "Where is the next Sleeper?"

There was a hollow silence, as if each of the others wanted someone else to say the name.

Then Mat spoke in a low voice filled with dread. "It's right in the center of the Forbidden Land!"

4

The Second Sleeper

From this point we must be very cautious. The Temple of the Sanhedrin is very close to where we're going."

Josh listened carefully as Crusoe spoke. They were resting their horses at the edge of a wild forest of ancient oaks. The great trees had been twisted into strange shapes by some unbelievable force.

The travelers were all mounted on sturdy ponies, except for Volka, who was too large for any horse. In addition, each led a packhorse laden with food, extra clothing, camping gear, and weapons.

For more than a week they had prepared for this journey. Then before dawn that very day, Crusoe had rousted them out and gotten them on the road. Since that early morning beginning, they had pushed on steadily, with only a brief stop for a quick meal at noon.

After midday, they left the highland and followed Crusoe into a tunnel of trees. The twisted branches of the oaks overhead nearly shut out the sun.

Finally, just as Josh was almost ready to fall out of the saddle, Crusoe called a halt. The riders climbed wearily off their horses and began to make camp.

It was then that Josh made a serious error.

He had gone into the woods for firewood. Suddenly a small animal darted in front of him. The animal looked much like a very small deer.

Now's my chance to bring home the first game, Josh thought. He unslung his bow, cocked an arrow, and for the first time he sent a barbed shaft through the air at a living thing.

Josh saw the arrow strike the small target. But before he could move, a hideous scream ripped through the forest. It was an unearthly noise that sounded like a woman's shrill, hysterical shriek.

"Look out! Look out!" the horrid voice cried.

Josh wheeled and ran blindly toward the camp. He ran so fast that he bumped into Mat, who fell sprawling.

The dwarf angrily spluttered, "What did you do?"

"Josh!" Crusoe came scurrying up. "Didn't I tell you we must make no noise! Come on, we must leave at once!"

As they scurried back to their mounts, Josh gasped, "What *was* it?"

"A look-out hart," Crusoe answered. "The Sanhedrin use them as an alarm system. They scream their heads off at anything unusual. After that, the Sanhedrin descend in force."

They reached the camp and began saddling the horses.

Josh was just thinking how lucky they were that the packs had not been unloaded when the shrill screaming stopped abruptly. Something, or somebody, was lurking at the edge of the camp. Josh glanced wildly around and saw that not one but many figures were standing in a circle around the campsite.

All of the strangers were tall, menacing creatures. Each wore a scarlet robe with a cowl that covered his face. A number in gold set inside a white circle gleamed on each breast. And there was a coldness in the air somehow that gripped Josh's heart like an icy fist. There was a sense of evil that he had never before felt.

Suddenly one of the strangers raised his hand and pointed at Crusoe. When he spoke, it was with a strange hollow tone.

"I am Elmas, Chief Interrogator and Servant of the Sanhedrin. Who are you, and why have you chosen to give up your lives by entering the Forbidden Land?"

Then Crusoe did something that Josh could not believe—he shrank into an even smaller shape, falling to the ground and crying and pleading in a high whine.

"No, Masters! Not the Forbidden Land. We've lost our way!" He began to sniffle and weep piteously. "We—we turned south two days ago so as to miss this place. We've lost our way. Please let us go! We're just poor folk trying to get to the village of Mantila."

"Quiet!" the hooded Chief Interrogator commanded. He turned his head and looked at each of them. Then his eyes lit on Josh, and he said suddenly, "Who is this one? He does not have the appearance of a Nuworlder."

Josh felt the burning eyes bore into his. He felt— *invaded*! Something had entered his mind and was beginning to strip him of everything.

He tried desperately to avoid the searcher. Then, as he stood helpless before the power that was beginning to possess him, there came a familiar voice that reminded him of what he must do—*"Be a half-wit."*

Instantly Josh threw himself to the ground, yelling the most idiotic things that occurred to him. He even frothed at the mouth. He screamed a series of phrases that poured out in meaningless patterns.

After a moment the Chief Interrogator said, "You may be the fools you seem to be, but you will appear at the Tower of Truth in the morning to undergo the Questioning."

He touched Crusoe on the forehead, and the old man went down as if he had been shot through the brain. The Chief Interrogator wheeled and amid a ghostly silence led the others out of the glen. In an instant, they had all faded into the depths of the forest.

49

Josh waited until he was certain they were gone. Then he stopped screaming and got up, trembling in every limb.

Crusoe had to be helped to his feet. When his eyes cleared, he said to Josh, "Now you know the power of the enemy!" Then the old man shook off their helping hands. "We must leave now—and ride all night. Quickly! Let us go."

The next few hours were like a bad dream. Already exhausted, Josh clung to the saddle only by an act of will as the travelers journeyed through the darkness of the forest.

Once they stopped to rest the animals. Only then did Crusoe ask, "Joshua, how did you ever think of using that crazy act? It was all that saved us."

The others all murmured agreement.

"Well, I . . ." Josh stammered, then he said defiantly, "A voice told me to do it." He waited for the hoot of derision, especially from Mat. Yet he saw only nods of agreement and a strange smile on Crusoe's face as they prepared to resume their journey.

Dawn was just turning the early morning skies to red when Crusoe led the group to a small canyon where there was a clear spring. They dismounted and drank deeply. After that, Josh saw Crusoe pull a rope out of his pack, walk to a tree, and sit down with his back to it. "Tie me to this tree," he said.

Josh watched in amazement as Mat and Tam lashed Crusoe so tightly that the ropes cut into his thin arms.

When he was firmly secured, Crusoe said, "Joshua, I think you should go away for a while."

"Why?" Josh asked.

"Because what is about to happen will be unpleasant. The Chief Interrogator commanded me to appear at the Tower. I will be forced to go there—*if I can!*" He nodded at his bonds. "These ropes will hold me until the spell passes."

Then Crusoe turned to the others. "Remember, no matter what I say or do—don't let me loose," he sternly instructed. "If you do, we'll all die."

Even as he spoke, a strange mad look came over his wrinkled face. He began speaking in a voice Josh had never heard before. "You can let me go. I'm all right now," Crusoe assured them.

He waited, then began to froth at the mouth and scream, fighting against the ropes. "Release me, you idiots! I must go to my masters! Release me at once!"

Josh watched transfixed, completely forgetting Crusoe's instructions to leave. He never forgot the nightmare he viewed. The old man was transformed into a beast that cried and begged, then cursed and blasphemed horribly. The seizure went on and on until he feared that Crusoe would die of convulsions.

Finally the old man slumped and expelled a huge sigh. When he lifted his head, his eyes were clear, and he said, "I am myself. You can release me when you think it wise."

Josh rushed forward. He drew his knife and cut Crusoe loose.

Tam offered their leader a drink of cool spring water.

Holding Crusoe in the circle of his arms while he drank and slowly recovered, Josh felt a strange sense of kinship with the twisted figure. Tears began to burn in his eyes.

Crusoe smiled through his wrinkles. He feebly patted Josh with a claw. "We are on our way, my boy."

"But where are we?" Mat murmured gloomily. "Is this the place?"

Crusoe slowly hobbled to his feet with Volka's help. "This is the location indicated by the song, but—sing it again, Josh. Maybe we'll get a better idea of the exact spot."

Josh sang the well-remembered words:

> *"'Far from ocean tides*
> *yet the Sleeper lies*

> *"'Where even sunlight seems to fail*
> *in the belly of the whale.'"*

There was a long silence.

Josh said, "I guess we'd better look for a whale."

"Great!" cried Tam happily. Then he added in a puzzled voice, "What's a whale?"

Josh started to explain, but Crusoe said, "Just spread out and look for anything *unusual*. If you find anything, sing out."

They separated and searched for several hours, finding nothing. Then Josh heard a whistle. When he finally located the source of the whistle, he also found the others. They were standing by a steel structure that was nearly covered with lichens.

"This must be it." Volka grinned. "But what *is* it? A water tank maybe?" He struck it with his huge fist, and an echo rang out. "Empty," the giant commented.

The structure was an oval steel tower rising about ten or twelve feet out of the sand. Try as they might, they could find no door or secret entrance.

"Sure doesn't look like a whale," Josh muttered. He glanced up and said, "Look at that."

He ran across the sand to a small mound rising out of the ground about fifty feet away. He cried out, "Hooray! Come and help me!" He began digging at the mound with his sword, sending the sand flying.

"What is it?" they all cried.

"Look!" Josh had uncovered a steel surface, and on it was a faded nameplate. He read aloud the words. *"USS Narwhale. It's a submarine,"* Josh explained. "Named after a whale. That's about as close as you can get to a whale on dry land, I guess."

"Yes—this *must* be what the song referred to," Crusoe said excitedly. "It must be an old war monument in a park. Or maybe there was an Oldworld river in this place."

"Come on," Josh said. "Let's get inside." They ran back to the exposed conning tower, and Josh turned to the giant. "Help me up to the top, Volka!" he begged.

The giant seized Josh and set him up on the structure. Then one by one, the others joined Josh as the giant helped them.

"I don't suppose I can get in the door," Volka said. "I'll keep watch while you're inside."

The plan sounded good, but they soon discovered that getting inside was not as easy as it looked. The steel hatch seemed to be welded to the deck. Not even Volka could have ripped it off.

They had tried everything they could think of and were beginning to argue bitterly about what to do, when Josh held up his hand. "Wait a minute. Be quiet."

They watched as Josh strained to hear a far-off voice. Then he said, "I remember something. Something I read in my mother's journal."

"What was it, Josh?" Crusoe asked quietly.

"Mom said, 'Sometimes, if everything else fails to solve a problem, you just speak to it. If you want to get rid of unforgiveness, say, 'Unforgiveness, get out of my heart.'"

"Well, what in the world does that mean?" Mat threw up his hands.

"I think," Josh said slowly, "that it means just what it says: Speak to *this* thing!"

53

"Oh, wonderful," Mat said mockingly. "You can talk to this thing—and I'll talk to the rocks. Tam can chat with the birdies, and—"

"Hush!" Crusoe said. "Do you believe it will happen, Josh?"

Josh said slowly, "I'll believe if you will."

"You're going to look like an idiot if nothing happens!" Mat warned. "What if you fail?"

Josh didn't answer. He merely took a deep breath and began to sing.

For a ghostly moment, nothing happened. Then, with a rusty groan, the hatch opened.

Relief and surprise washed over Josh. With a gesture to the others, he scrambled down inside. His friends quickly followed.

They found the capsule with ease, but, strangely, indecision seemed to seize Josh even as this part of his quest was ending. Finally, with a nod from Crusoe, he pushed the button and stepped closer for his first glimpse of the waiting sleeper.

5

Trust the Heart

S arah!" Josh said in amazement—and some disappointment. He suddenly realized how desperately he had
hoped that this Sleeper would be a strong leader.

Mat evidently felt the same. "You know this one?
Humph! Well, it's just another baby—and a female at
that!"

"But a *pretty* one." Tam beamed. Both he and Crusoe
leaned closer to get a good look at Sarah.

When one is rudely awakened and sees two hairy
dwarfs and an ugly hunchback not two feet away—well,
what does one do?

Scream, of course! And the poor girl did exactly that,
throwing herself into the arms of the startled Josh. He
was torn by two emotions—terribly disappointed that no
leader had emerged, yet finding it pleasant to hold the slim
girl in his arms.

It made him feel so masculine that he said, rather ar-
rogantly, "Back up there, you fellows—give her a chance
to breathe!"

He was a little surprised when they obeyed instantly,
so he said even louder, "Come on, Sarah. I'll explain
everything to you later. Right now we've got to get out of
here."

As Josh led them to the door, Sarah clung closely to
him, and he did not protest. Instead he said with newfound authority, "Step lively, men—be alert!"

Tam could not resist giving a mock salute and saying,
"Right you are, sir. Yes, sir!" as they made their exit.

Then Josh, feeling a great deal like some romantic sea captain, went one step too far. "Here you go, Sarah," he said, and with what he hoped looked like a dashing gesture, he half-lifted and half-pushed Sarah over the side of the tower.

He had forgotten two things. One was that Sarah did not know that she was going to be thrown off a building. Second, she did not expect to be caught in the hairy arms of a potato-faced giant with a sinister, gap-tooth grin.

Therefore, when she plunged over the side and the giant caught her and held her tight in his muscular arms, she let out some really earth-shattering screams—loud enough to alert any Sanhedrin up to two miles away.

Crusoe said instantly, "Shut her up, Volka! Carry her to cover—and keep her quiet!"

Like frightened rabbits, the group scrambled to the ground and scurried back to the grove. There they fell to the earth, gasping for breath.

All except Sarah. Since Volka had carried her, she had plenty of breath. She began to use it immediately on the unfortunate Josh.

"Josh Adams! I can't believe anyone could be so dumb!"

"But I—"

"You—I—you! I'm so mad I could spit!" Sarah sputtered. "When you woke up, did someone throw you off a building—to a—a monster?"

Volka grinned broadly and shook his head.

"Well, no," Josh stammered, "but—"

"I never want to speak to you again as long as I live!" Sarah said fiercely.

She probably did not really mean this, but Josh believed her. His shoulders slumped, his face went red, and he felt totally humiliated.

"*Ahem!*" Crusoe broke in with a slight cough. "May I have a quiet word with you, Miss—Sarah, is it?" The old man had a nice smile in spite of his ruined face, and he turned it on the angry girl.

Sarah looked at him, then nodded with a very small smile of her own.

"Suppose you and I go for a short walk, and I'll attempt to clear this up," Crusoe suggested. As they turned to go, he spoke to the others. "Why don't you fix something to eat? And Josh" —he lowered his voice— "don't worry, my boy. She'll get over it."

"Who cares!" Josh simmered. "She always was a stuck-up snob." He pretended to ignore the pair as they left.

Tam chose that moment to give the unfortunate boy one more jab.

"Any more orders, Captain?" He gave his silly salute again.

At last Josh found an outlet for his frustration. Without a word, he leaped on the startled Tam. They started an awkward scuffle, kicking and flailing in the dust.

"Maybe I ought to stop them," Volka said to Mat.

"Let them fight," Mat growled. "Maybe they'll kill each other—or at least beat some sense into their dull heads. But I doubt it."

By the time Crusoe led Sarah back to camp, Tam and Josh had made their peace. The food was nearly cooked too—sizzling steaks and steaming potatoes. There was even a portion of crusty bread dripping in butter for each of them.

Evidently Sarah had changed her mind, for she walked right up to Josh. "Josh, I'm sorry I acted so rotten. I won't act that way anymore," she promised. She waited a moment, then put her small hand on his arm and said softly, "Won't you forgive me, Josh?"

Turning very red, Josh finally muttered, "Sure, yeah." Then he hastily shoved a huge piece of buttered bread into his mouth to cover his awkwardness. However, he did look pleased when Sarah got her food and came back to sit close to him.

They sat up far into the night. The fire and the danger seemed to make them all feel very close.

For two days they rested, keeping careful watch for the Sanhedrin. Then they resumed their journey in short trips. Several times Josh thought he saw the red robes of the Servants in the distance, but he was never sure.

This went on for three weeks. Josh seemed to be growing stronger every day—not only physically but emotionally. His terrible self-consciousness was fading. It was Josh, more often than not, who made the decision to go forward or to camp.

One morning at breakfast, Crusoe made the inevitable announcement. "Well, the food is gone—but we'll be at the spot by early afternoon if all goes well." Then he noticed that Sarah was only picking at her food.

"What's the matter, child?"

"Oh, nothing . . ." She hesitated. "Yes, there is something the matter, but I—I'm not sure I can tell you about it."

"I think we've come far enough to tell each other anything," Josh said.

Sarah smiled at him. "Well, all right. After you all went to sleep last night, a man came into the camp."

Immediately they all protested that it could not be. "Impossible! Can't be! We would have heard him!" And so on.

"You were all sound asleep—and I almost was, but then I looked up and there he was, right in front of me, with his back to the fire." She paused and thought for a moment, her face intent. "The funny thing was, I wasn't afraid! There he was, a murderer for all I knew, and yet I had the strangest sense that he was—safe. That's the only way I can put it."

"Did he say anything?" Crusoe asked.

"Yes," Sarah nodded. "First he said, 'Sarah, don't be afraid.' Then he said, 'When all fails, trust your heart.'"

Mat threw his hands in the air and barked, "Just what we need—another mystic prophet spouting poetry!"

"Hush, Mat," Crusoe commanded. "Did he say anything else?"

"Well, I asked him his name. He said, just before he faded into the trees, 'Very soon you will know my name.'"

Sarah looked around. "Don't you believe me—any of you?"

Volka grinned. "I do!" he declared.

"So do I," cried Tam, who had so much affection for Sarah that he would have believed her if she had said that the sun was made of taffy.

Then Josh grinned. He—the one who heard voices no one else could hear—was a fine one to doubt. "I believe you, Sarah."

Crusoe warmly added, "We all do."

Mat made a show of protest. "Humbug! Last dwarf I knew who trusted his heart died in a lunatic asylum!"

Nevertheless, he winked slyly and gently pinched Sarah on the arm.

* * *

Shortly after dawn, the company stopped, hid the horses in a large clump of maples, and began the search.

"What do we look for?" Tam asked.

Josh said, "Well, the song gives us the only hint.

"'Where the sweetest breath
turns to sudden death—

"'There the son of Isaac sleeps.'

"Maybe it'll get clearer, but I guess we'll just spread out and try to find something unusual. Sarah, you come with me."

By noon they had walked for miles. Their faces were scratched by briars, their feet sore. They gathered under a large bush, completely discouraged.

"This is no good," Mat moaned.

"No, we could search for months," Crusoe agreed. He looked wearily at the rock-covered landscape. "We'd better make a permanent camp in a better place."

They were almost back to the ponies when suddenly Sarah stopped. "Wait a minute. I just thought of something. That man I saw last night—he may be the key to finding the Sleeper."

"Romantic nonsense. Not scientific," Mat grumbled shortly.

"But what if he meant it literally—I mean really literally?"

"Well—" Crusoe chuckled a little "—if we're going to trust a prophet, I think we'd better trust him all the way —or not at all."

"But how can we do it?" Josh asked.

Sarah touched the gold chain that she wore and drew out a locket engraved with an emblem. "When I woke up, I had this on," she said.

They all drew close and stared at the necklace.

"It's a gold heart!" Josh cried out.

"I don't think it's gold," Sarah said, "but I think this is the heart that the man meant. See how dull it is."

The heart was covered with a dull yellow film.

"But I noticed when we were over in that direction it was very shiny and bright."

"Well, what do you think that means?" Mat asked.

"I think the heart is—well—not magic exactly, but somehow it gets bright when it's close to a Sleeper and dull when it's far off."

"A good inventor could probably make it sensitive to some metal in the capsules," Crusoe mused. "Maybe this is a time to trust the heart."

"I never heard such rot!" Mat scoffed. "Why, you can't take prophecies and signs literally."

"Yes, we can," Josh said. "What else do we have? Come on, it's worth a try."

They began to retrace their steps.

Before they had covered half a mile, Sarah cried out. "Look—the heart, it's getting bright!"

They needed no other sign but doubled their pace. Josh forgot all his weariness.

"You know what, Josh?" Sarah asked.

"What?"

"I wish I knew his name—the man I saw last night."

"Well—" Josh smiled "—he was right about the heart. Guess you can trust him to do what he said about the name."

"Yes. He did say, 'Soon you'll know my name.'"

Josh trudged on silently, then said, "Sarah, when you find out his name, tell me, will you?"

6

A Taste of Honey

I never saw a tree like that before," Josh said. The group had been following the path set by Sarah's golden heart when they came across a strange, stunted tree. He stopped and peered upward. Brown fruit hung from its top branches.

"I have," Volka said. "It's a honeyfruit tree. Here, try some." He picked some fruit and tossed it to them. "The bees stuff honey in the fruit for some reason."

"It's crisp and delicious," Sarah said, licking her fingers. "Let's take as much as we can with us."

So they did. Volka stripped the branches, and all filled their pockets and packs.

It wasn't long before Josh said, "Look, there's a hummingbird—and there's another!"

"Wait a minute," Tam said suddenly. "Those aren't hummingbirds—they're bees!" He ducked as one rifled by his head. "They're bigger than sparrows!"

"Be careful," Crusoe warned. "I saw one of those sting a dog once, and he died in a few hours."

"Look," Sarah said, "I don't see how the heart could be any brighter! We must be close."

"Hey," Josh called out, pointing at an opening in a large rock formation that rose twenty or thirty feet in the air. "That must be it. Come on!"

He started to run to the opening, but Mat tripped him neatly, spilling him on the ground. Josh got up angrily. "Why'd you do that?" he spluttered.

Mat pointed at the opening. "Look at that. See those bees going in and coming out? That whole rock is a beehive for those monsters!"

Crusoe nodded. "I think you're right. And it would be suicide to go in there! Let's see if we can find another opening."

They skirted the rock formation, but there was no other opening. They tried walking away, but the heart at once began to lose its fire and grow dull.

"That's it, I guess," Tam said. "Can't we smoke them out?"

"Too big," Mat answered. "We'll have to go back until we can think of something. We can't go in there."

"I believe if we've been led this far, we're intended to go in," said Sarah sharply. "What do you think, Josh?" She turned to him for support.

What neither Sarah nor any of the others could know was that Joshua, who was not in the least fearful of a snake or a spider, was terrified of bees and wasps. In fact, he was allergic to them. Once, when he was eight years old, he had been stung by a honeybee. The convulsions that followed nearly killed him. Ever since then, Josh had been almost helplessly terrified of bees.

In response to Sarah's question, he only reddened and mumbled. "Well, maybe Mat is right. Some things are too hard."

Sarah seemed caught off guard. She looked at Josh a little closer, but he ducked his head.

"Well, I'm going in," Sarah said.

"I'll go with you," Crusoe declared. "We'll be all right if we don't accidentally mash one of them. That sends off a warning to attack, and we'd be dead right off."

The pair walked toward the door.

* * *

Crouching low, Sarah and Crusoe advanced down a tunnel that must have been seven feet high and at least three feet wide. Overhead Sarah heard the zinging sound of the bees going in and out of the hive. They had not gone far when it grew too dark to see.

"This won't do," Crusoe said. "We may blunder into some grubs in this blasted darkness." Then he looked over his shoulder. "What's that?"

A light was coming down the tunnel behind them. Soon Sarah heard Josh's voice.

"It's me. I'm—I'm coming with you." His voice trembled, and the light in his hand was unsteady.

Crusoe threw his arm about Josh's shoulders—something he had never done before. He whispered huskily, "I know how hard this is for you, my boy."

Sarah squeezed Josh's hand.

The trio had gone only a few steps farther when suddenly Josh stopped and said, "Listen to that!"

The air, Sarah realized, was filled with a tremendous humming, like a mighty dynamo.

Josh threw his light on the walls. They had entered a large cavern. The walls were all honeycombs, swarming with thousands and thousands of the giant bees. It was the bees that made the terrible humming.

"Come on," Josh said. "I think there's an opening . . ." Suddenly he yelled.

In the dim light Sarah saw that a great bee had lighted on the helpless Josh. Its needlelike stinger was ready to sink into his neck.

"Don't move, Josh!" Crusoe said instantly. "Don't move a muscle."

Somehow Josh was able to obey. Finally, after what had to have been some of the longest moments of his life, the bee flew off.

"Josh!" Sarah grabbed his arm. "Are you all right?"

"I—think so," Josh said unevenly. "But it was so odd! That thing lit on my neck, and I almost jumped out of my skin. Then—well, it was like I was lifted out of my body and someone else stepped in and sort of became me. And then the bee went off, and I came back! What does it mean?" he asked Crusoe.

The old man shrugged, but there was a strange fire in his eyes. "We are not alone, are we, my boy?"

The three slowly continued on their way. Just as they were about to leave the immense central cavern, Sarah spoke. "Smell that? It's the honey."

"Like the song, *'Where the sweetest breath'* —that's the honey— *'turns to sudden death,'* that's the bees."

They entered a much smaller tunnel. At the end of the passage, they found what they were seeking—a white door that opened when the song was sung. Inside stood the third capsule, full of the dense gas.

As they stood before it, Crusoe looked at Josh. He asked curiously, "Do you expect to find a great captain in this one?"

Josh did not smile. "It will be whoever it should be." He pushed the button marked AWAKE, and the chamber cleared slowly. The top swung open.

They watched as an undersized, red-haired teenager opened his eyes and sat up.

When the Sleeper saw the travelers, he jumped off the bed and put his back to the wall. "Who are you?" he asked defiantly.

"Friends," Sarah said. "I'm Sarah, this is Josh, and that is Crusoe."

The small redhead had a pug nose, and there was a fighting light in his bright eyes.

"How do I know you're not enemies?" he demanded.

"Well," Josh said, "why don't you test us—ask us questions?"

"OK, I will. What's a Big Mac?"

"A hamburger!" Josh and Sarah answered.

"Who was Humphrey Bogart?"

"A great film star."

"What's General Motors?"

"A car company."

Slowly a grin broke across the face of the redhead. He admitted, "Well, I guess only real Americans would know that stuff. You can call me Jake. Jake Garfield."

"A 'son of Isaac,'" Crusoe murmured.

"That's right," Jake said. "My old man's name *was* Isaac, but how'd you figure that?"

"We'll tell you when we get out of here, Jake. Let's go."

They found their way out without incident, though Jake's eyes bulged at the massive bees. He seemed even more amazed at the sight of a giant and a pair of dwarfs.

"Are you *sure* they're all friendly?" he whispered to Josh as he gazed at Volka. "I'd hate to have to mess with that guy!"

Later that night the company ate the last of the honeyfruit. As they ate, Crusoe told Jake the history of the Sleepers. He also told him of the Quest.

Then Jake looked around the campfire and grinned broadly. "Well, we got one tough, if a bit small, lady; one beanpole on his way to manhood; one hunchback; one hairless King Kong; two midgets; and a skinny redhead. I don't see why we can't save the world with such a pack."

He looked so satisfied that they all had to laugh at his cocky attitude.

"Where do we go from here?" Jake asked.

"Well, here's the song," Josh said.

"All caves of earth are dark and drear,
  except the one that glows like diamonds clear.

"'He who would this Sleeper wake,
  must pass the deadly jaws of fate.'

"There's 18 syllables in the first group—and 15 in the second. Let's see," Josh murmured.

They gathered around the worn map, and Crusoe whistled as Josh put his finger on the spot.

"This won't be easy," Crusoe remarked. "Look, if we go this way down the Temple Road, we're almost sure to be recognized. But the other way is right back through the Forbidden Land."

"Not that way!" they all said at once.

"No, it's too dangerous," Crusoe agreed. "There's only one other way that I can see. Look, we can get a boat right here and sail south through the Dark Sea."

"Not *there,*" Mat said. "That's the Ghost Marshes. *Nobody* goes through there."

"Why not?" Josh asked.

"For one thing—merely a small detail, you understand—people go in on one side and never come out on the other. Sorry to be so picky." Mat sniffed disdainfully. "Of course, in this group of mystics, someone will probably *dream* us across the Marsh!"

After much argument, the travelers finally agreed that there was no other way. They would have to find a boat and pass through the Ghost Marshes.

7

The Ghost Marshes

Although getting from their camp to the sea was no problem, finding a boat was a different matter. While most of the group waited a short distance from the shore, Crusoe and Josh set out to buy or borrow a boat.

After several failures, they met a fisherman named Dedron who said that he would sell them one of his old boats.

"Not good for fishing much," Dedron said in some sort of mixed dialect.

After looking at the boat, Crusoe said it would suffice for one voyage. "We'll take it," he told Dedron and handed him several gold coins as payment.

Dedron, a large and homely man with a fisherman's scarred hands and weathered skin, looked curiously at the coins, then said, "First money I see in two years." He held up three dirty fingers to clarify his speech.

"Why is that?" Josh asked. "Can't you sell your fish?"

Dedron held out a muscular forearm for them to see. "No have mark," he said. "Cannot buy or sell." He shot a question at them. "Do *you* have mark to buy and sell?"

Josh looked at Crusoe, who said, "No. Neither of us."

The fisherman looked at them as if weighing them in a careful balance. "I put my life in your hands—are you in the House?"

"In the house?" Josh asked. "What does that mean?"

Dedron rumbled, "You not know song? I sing it for you."

In a voice completely off-key, he sang a song that shocked Josh to the bone—the same words that Josh's father had sung in another world, in another time.

> *"The House of Goél will be filled,*
> *The earth itself will quake!*
> *The Beast will be forever stilled*
> *When Seven Sleepers wake!"*

"But what does it mean?" Josh asked. "Who is Goél, and who is the Beast—and who are the Seven Sleepers?"

"I am only fisherman," Dedron said, shrugging his shoulders. "But I think it mean that one day—soon—bad men will all be killed and good man will come. And then all the world be happy."

"But who sings this song? And how did you learn it?" Crusoe asked.

"I know it all my life." Dedron shrugged again. "But now, lots of people sing it. Not when Sanhedrin is near, but at night in secret places."

Crusoe breathed quickly. "Do you hear that, Josh? That's the Uprising the Sanhedrin is trying to stamp out. And it sounds like it's spreading faster than they can get rid of it."

Crusoe turned once more to Dedron and asked, "When will all this happen?"

Dedron looked at him impatiently. "Listen to song— *'When Seven Sleepers wake.'* Maybe soon. Then House of Goél be filled!"

He shoved the coins back into Crusoe's hand. "No pay—we brothers. Anyway, I no can spend."

They heard him laughing as they hurried back to camp.

When the two reached camp, Josh was at first so filled with their news that he noticed nothing unusual. No sooner had they got in voice range than he cried out, "We've found out about the Uprising and about the Seven Sleepers!"

Just as he was about to launch into his story, Josh saw Mat gesturing with his head toward a clump of trees. Josh realized then that Mat's hands and feet were tied! Everyone was tied up!

A scarlet-clad figure stepped from behind a giant elm. It was Elmas, the Chief Interrogator, who had met them in the forest.

Josh tried to run, but a single "Stop!" from Elmas froze him in his tracks.

"Bind them, Onar. I will take these two in the chariot to the Temple for the Questioning," he said, indicating Tam and Jake. "An armed escort will be sent for you and the rest. You will guard them well. On your life, Onar."

There was a clear threat in Elmas's muffled voice.

Onar answered at once, "Yes, Master."

Onar threw Tam and Jake into the chariot, cuffing them into silence when they tried to speak to the others. Then Elmas got in and, without a word, picked up the whip and lashed the horses into a dead run down the road.

"How long will it take the escort to get here?" Josh whispered to Crusoe.

"About four hours—unless he meets a patrol already on the march. We've got to get loose."

"Quiet!" Onar suddenly stood over them. "You will not speak." Then he looked at Crusoe and said, "Maybe you will talk. There is much that you can tell me before the Master returns. What is your name, Old One?"

Crusoe tightened his lips and made no answer.

His silence seemed to infuriate Onar. He seized the frail hunchback and carried him toward a clump of trees almost as easily as Volka would have done. When the pair was concealed by the thicket, Josh heard Onar ask a question and pause. Then, instead of an answer, there was the sound of a blow being struck—then another, and many more.

"He'll kill Crusoe," Mat whispered in a fury. "Can't any of you get loose?"

"I can't," Sarah said.

Volka groaned. "No, too tight."

Perhaps Onar had been in too much of a hurry, but Josh felt a slackness in the ropes around his wrists. He gasped with effort and was almost free when Mat warned him, "Watch out, Josh! He's coming."

The hulking figure came toward them, carrying the limp body of Crusoe. He threw him down with a curse. "Stubborn fool!"

Then his eyes lit on Sarah. He moved toward her and jerked her to her feet. "Maybe you will be more talkative," he said. He moved with the frightened girl, now helpless in his grasp, toward the trees.

"No!" Josh cried.

Onar glanced at him with an evil grin. "Don't worry, boy, your time is coming—and you'll be begging me to take her instead of you!"

He laughed cruelly as he moved to the trees, but this time he was not concealed. His broad back was just visible.

Josh grunted fiercely, and his hands finally broke free. At the same time, he heard Sarah cry out in pain. Blind with rage, Josh started to run to her aid, but Mat's whisper stopped him.

"No, Josh! You won't have a chance! The bow! Josh, the bow!"

Mat nodded at a nearby tree, and Josh saw Onar's bow and a full quiver of hunting arrows. He seized the bow and strung it in one smooth motion. Then he cocked an arrow and pulled it to his cheek. Suddenly he paused.

"Shoot! Shoot!" Mat urged.

Josh had never loved hunting, though he had often accompanied his father on trips. Looking at Onar's back, he realized that he was about to take a human life. Everything in his past said no.

Yet, even as he wavered, Sarah cried out again.

Mat whispered desperately, "They'll kill Sarah, Josh. They'll kill all of us, if you don't get us away from here! And you can't do it as long as Onar is alive!"

Perhaps even this would not have been enough, but then there came into Josh's mind the same faint voice that he had heard once before. He heard the words again, *The House of Goél must be filled.*

Josh set his jaw and sent the arrow right through Onar's broad back. The Servant grunted once, then fell forward.

Josh ran and pulled the scarlet-clad form away from Sarah.

"Come on. It's all right now, but we have to hurry," he urged.

As he pulled her away, Josh took one clear look at the blood that stained the ground around Onar. He realized that he had lost something very precious. Never again, he knew, could he be the simple boy that he had been.

They freed the others quickly.

"What are we going to do about Tam and Jake?" Sarah asked.

"We can't help them by staying here," Josh said. "We'll find some way to get them back later."

"Where are we going?" Sarah asked as they moved toward the sea.

Volka was carrying the limp form of Crusoe. The others carried the supplies.

"We're going to the boat, then to the next Sleeper." Josh spoke with a hard tone. Onar's death had changed him.

He got them to the boat and, when they were ready, shoved off. Mat knew a little about sailing, so he took control of the small craft.

"How is he?" Josh finally asked, as Sarah leaned over Crusoe.

"He's unconscious," she said. "I—I think he's hurt *very* badly. Can't we get a doctor?"

"I don't see how," Josh said grimly. "Do you know any medicine, Mat?"

"If I did, I'd use it on myself," Mat said.

Then Josh noticed that Mat was swaying on the seat, pale as ashes.

"What's wrong?" Josh sprang to help him, and the dwarf slumped to the bottom of the boat. "I'm a Gemini—that's what's wrong."

And then Josh remembered what Crusoe had said— that Gemini twins would die if separated.

"You'll be all right soon, Mat," Josh encouraged him. "They're taking Tam to the Temple, and that's where we're headed too—in a roundabout way."

Mat brightened a little. "We are? That's good. I don't feel so well." Then he fainted.

So there they were. Two dying men, two teenagers, and a giant.

* * *

It was nearly dark when Mat awoke and pulled himself up to look over the side. "That's it," he whispered. "That's the sea entrance to the Ghost Marshes."

Somehow they landed, and then Volka had his finest hour. They could not have done it without the giant, for he practically carried them all on his broad back. "Load me up!" he said with a swagger. "I've never seen a load I couldn't carry!"

They tied Mat in a sling on Volka's back, then hung

the supplies and packs anywhere they could. Volka picked Crusoe up in his arms. Loaded like a frigate, he plowed into the muck of the evil-smelling swamp. He called to Sarah and Josh. "Catch hold and come on, young ones! I'm Volka, and no little swamp stops me!"

Forever after on that trip, when any of them was in trouble, Josh would remind himself that nothing could be as bad as the Ghost Marshes. For hours they slogged through the sucking mud. They finally gave up trying to wave away the bloodthirsty mosquitoes. They exhausted all their strength, then summoned still more.

It was not just a terrible physical effort. Josh thought there was something evil and hungry about the way the mud tried to suck them under, as if it were trying to devour them.

And there were voices that whispered, "Rest a little! You're so tired! Just for a moment, then you'll be stronger."

Finally even Volka was swaying from side to side, about to topple with his burdens. At last they all slumped in a helpless sprawl beside a huge cypress.

And the voices sounded so good that, one by one, each of the weary travelers slipped into a drugged sleep.

What would have happened if they had continued sleeping, Josh never knew. Only a familiar voice that stirred in his mind kept him from finding out.

"Joshua, you must get up," the voice urged.

He tried to ignore the words, but the voice came again, sternly this time. *"Joshua, I need you."*

Josh slowly and painfully opened his eyes. There before him in the shadows of the swamp was a tall figure dressed in rough brown cloth, his face shielded by a hood.

"You must awaken the others and follow me," he said.

Josh staggered to his feet. Somehow he got them all awake, and they staggered out of the swamp.

"Where are we going, Josh?" Sarah asked weakly.

"Out of here—where he says," Josh said, pointing at the tall figure going before them.

But Sarah seemed not to see the man.

Finally they stumbled out of the mud onto firm land. The sky opened up, and fields appeared.

Suddenly Josh felt someone near and turned to find the tall man beside him pointing at something.

"That is where you are to go, Joshua," he said. He would have passed on then, into the woods, but Joshua called after him.

"Who are you?" he cried. "What's your name?"

The man was almost invisible in the darkness of the trees, but he turned and spoke clearly.

"Yes, you have earned the right to know my name."

He turned, and as he disappeared in the morning mists he called back in a clear voice, *"I am Goél!"*

Then he was gone.

Josh stood and listened to the echo of that name.

8

The Fourth Sleeper

Josh peered into the darkness of the woods so long that he was startled when Sarah came up behind him.

"What is it, Josh?"

"Oh! I was just wondering . . ." Josh began. Then for some reason he felt powerless to mention the stranger. He said instead, "Look, there's the place. At least I think so."

He pointed to a large steel door set in a hillside about a hundred yards away from where they stood.

Sarah pulled her necklace free. As they walked toward the cave, she said, "You must be right. Look how the heart is glowing."

Without hesitation they walked up to the massive door. Josh immediately recited the song.

> *"All caves of earth are dark and drear,*
> *except that one that glows like diamonds clear.*

> *"'He who would this Sleeper wake,*
> *must pass the deadly jaws of fate.'"*

Suddenly the door separated like a set of huge fangs. The top half slid up, and the bottom half lowered, revealing diamond-shaped teeth that met.

"They're *jaws*! Just like a shark," Sarah said.

"Come on, Sarah," Josh said. "Volka, you rest here and take care of the others." Josh indicated the still unconscious Crusoe and Mat, and the giant wearily nodded. Then Josh and Sarah slipped through the dangerous opening.

Josh had expected the cave to be as dark as the hive had been. Therefore, he was amazed to see that a brilliant light illuminated the cavern, making it even brighter than daylight.

"What is it?" Sarah asked breathlessly. "I've never seen anything so beautiful! It's like a million Christmas trees all at once!"

"Sure is," Josh whispered. He blinked. The walls and roof glittered as if they were studded with precious stones —green emeralds, glowing red rubies, flashing diamonds.

Josh touched the walls carefully. "I think it's some kind of quartz formation," he said. He did not know really, but the words sounded impressive.

"Let's hurry. We've got to get back to the others," Sarah said.

Finding the Sleeper was not difficult. The familiar capsule lay open to view in a small chamber. As they had done before, they paused to activate the system that would awake the person who lay resting inside.

Sarah said, "Josh, I have a feeling that this Sleeper is really something. I mean," she tried to explain, "it's just got to be, hasn't it?"

Josh knew what she meant. "Yeah, we're in such a mess now it'll take a real *somebody* to do us any good. Well, push the button, Sarah. Keep your fingers crossed, and hope it'll be a super person!"

After Sarah had pushed the button, they waited for the vapor to clear. When it did, they both gasped as the plastic hood swung free.

"Oh!" Sarah breathed. "I think we really did find a super person!"

The Sleeper who opened his eyes and slowly sat up was one of the handsomest boys that Josh had ever seen.

He was perhaps a year older than Josh. Everything about him seemed perfect, from his clear skin and perfectly formed head to his trim athletic figure. He looked like one of those young men that Josh had always envied in Old-world because they could always win at any game or find a ready audience.

Perhaps this bitter memory set Josh to wondering what good another teenager—and probably a spoiled one, at that—was going to be on the Quest. But as he greeted the Sleeper, Josh tried to hide his thoughts. He smiled quickly and said, "Hello. I'm Josh Adams, and this is Sarah Collingwood."

"I'm Dave Cooper," replied the Sleeper.

They shook hands awkwardly.

After a pause, Dave prompted, "Well, I guess you'll have to tell me what's going on."

Sarah began to explain.

Josh grumpily thought that she elaborated and exaggerated too much. *Showing off,* he thought.

"You see, Dave, there are seven of us, we think," Sarah was saying. "We have to wake up all of them. Now that there are four of us—"

"Where's the other one?" Dave asked.

"Well, a man named Elmas—wait a minute, I'll have to tell you about the Sanhedrin—"

"We'd better get to the others," Josh interrupted. "It's going to take a while to tell all this. You can tell it as we go, Sarah."

They left the capsule and made their way toward the Jaws of Fate. Sarah led the way, rapidly telling Dave all the story. Josh trailed behind.

When they got to the Jaws of Fate, Dave and Sarah passed through easily, but just as Josh cleared the opening, the Jaws snapped together, barely missing him.

"What—what was *that?*" Dave whispered, swallow-ing as he stared at the massive steel teeth.

"Oh, nothing," Josh said casually, though his voice was not quite steady. "Let's get going."

By the time they reached the others, Sarah had ex-plained the Quest to Dave.

She had also prepared him for what he would see. Thus Dave showed no fear when Volka suddenly stepped toward them.

The giant grunted. "I see you got him."

"How's Crusoe?" Josh asked at once. "And Mat?"

"I think Mat is better. Crusoe—not so good."

The old man, in fact, looked terrible. He was pale, and his heart seemed to be skipping a beat now and then.

Josh said worriedly, "He's really sick. I don't see how we can travel until he gets better. He needs some rest and something to eat."

Josh tried to think, but the ordeal in the Ghost Marsh had drained him mentally as well as physically. "I just don't know *what* to do," he muttered wearily and slumped to the ground.

None of the group spoke for a moment.

Then Dave said slowly, "Well, of course I'm in the dark about most of this, but you all look beat to me. I don't think any of you could get very far without some rest and food—especially Mr. Crusoe."

"We *know* that. I just said so," Josh snapped. "Where can we get something to eat? That's what we need to know."

"From the cave," Dave said. "Didn't you see the room next to where I was? They showed it to me before I went to sleep."

"I didn't notice," Josh said, trying to dismiss the information.

"It's full of all kinds of stuff—food, clothes, supplies."

80

The others began to look a little more encouraged.

"Say," Dave said, suddenly, "I've got an idea! Why don't we go back and stay in the cave? It's safe there—especially with those jaws! And we can rest and get some food inside us. I'm starving, myself."

Dave organized them into some kind of order, with Volka carrying Crusoe, and the rest taking the few supplies. Soon they were moving toward the cave.

Sarah pulled at Josh's arm.

"Dave is pretty super after all, isn't he? He sure learned everything quickly enough. And now he thought of the cave. I think we'll be all right now."

"It's going to take more than Mr. Wonderful to get us through," Josh grumped.

Sarah looked at him in amazement. "What's wrong? Don't you like Dave?"

Josh could not answer honestly. He was a little envious at the easy way that the other boy had taken command.

"I'm just tired," he muttered. He was about to say more when Sarah left him, running ahead to walk beside Dave.

They entered the Jaws of Fate and soon had a cheery fire going. They fixed chocolate, and toast covered with cheese. There was some soup for Crusoe, who was beginning to show much more life, and there was a variety of canned meat. Some chocolate chip cookies in sealed bags had survived the years quite well.

After they could eat no more, the travelers rolled themselves into warm sleeping bags. The last thing Josh remembered before he plunged into the soundest sleep he had ever known was Sarah and Dave talking.

* * *

When Josh finally awakened, he found himself caught up in a plan that Dave had devised with some help from Sarah.

Dave was quick to ask Josh's opinion, but it was immediately clear that the others had already agreed to try the plan.

"You were really worn out, Josh," Dave said sympathetically. "I knew you'd be anxious to get on the way, so here's what we've decided. Here's the next Sleeper." He pulled out the worn map.

Josh looked at him sharply, and Dave added, "We didn't want to disturb you, so I took it out of your pocket. I hope you don't mind."

As a matter of fact, Josh did mind, but what could he say?

"It's so simple," Dave went on. "You've already come through the worst of the country. Now all we have to do is get out of these woods and hit the Great Road —see?"

"I know that," Josh snapped. "But it may not be so easy."

"All we have to do is hit the Great Road, and it leads right to the city. That's where the next Sleeper lies. What could be easier? You'll think more clearly when you're a little more awake," Dave added loftily.

"I'm awake enough to know that the Sanhedrin has an alarm out for us! How long do you think it'll take them to spot us on that highway out in the open?"

"Say, that's right," Mat said. "We have to keep away from the main road."

Dave waved his hand airily and showed his perfect teeth in a big smile. "Don't worry! When we get there, we'll skirt the roads. The important thing is to keep *moving*. Come on, let's go."

Josh had time to speak to Crusoe for only a minute before Volka picked the old man up. "How do you feel? If you can't make it, we'll stay here until you're better."

"Sorry to be such a bother, Josh—but I do feel much better," Crusoe assured him. "As long as we're careful, we should be all right. But keep your eyes on that young man." Crusoe pointed at Dave. "He could get us captured if he doesn't learn caution."

"I'll watch him all right—but it seems like everyone is convinced that he's the great leader," Josh said grimly.

He glanced jealously at Sarah. Dave was helping her place her pack just right, and Josh thought that she looked far too happy.

They left the edge of the Ghost Marshes, and at once the country began to flatten out. They followed a broad trail evidently used by many travelers. They covered a quarter of the distance to the Great Road before they stopped for lunch. After a quick meal and a short rest, they continued.

By afternoon, Josh had decided that he had been wrong and Dave had been right. Grudgingly, he began to admit to himself that maybe Dave was the leader they needed.

But his thoughts were abruptly interrupted when he heard Volka shout, "Everyone watch out—*Snakepeople!*"

Volka put Crusoe down and set himself for a fight.

Out of a canyon came a number of terrifying creatures—perhaps twenty in all. They were upon the small group so fast that Josh had time for only a quick glimpse before the attack.

He whipped out his sword as if he'd been doing it all his life and plunged it into the scaly breast of one of the creatures. The thing was not really human, although it had two legs and two arms, for the limbs and the body were truly snakelike, twisting and writhing in coils.

The worst part of the creature was its head. Instead of a human face, it had a pointed surface with black beady eyes and a mouth with two large fangs. From the fangs dripped some sort of clear fluid.

Josh no sooner dropped the first creature than another attacked. The little group was indeed hard pressed by the attackers.

In the heat of the crisis, Dave showed his true ability to organize. He was fighting off some of the Snakepeople with a sword that Mat had given him, and still managing to shout directions and encouragement to the others. "Get back against this bluff, everyone. Look out, Mat, there's one behind you! Get those bows in action!"

It was Volka who gave them time to form, for with a roar and one blow of his massive forearm, he swept aside half a dozen of the horrible creatures. This allowed Mat and Sarah to use their bows. As another enemy wave swept toward them, Josh heard the hiss and impact of arrows striking home. Sarah was not hitting much, but Mat proved to be a deadly marksman. Soon the bodies of the snakelike creatures were littering the ground.

"There's too many of them!" Josh shouted as he fended off two scaly bodies at once with his blade. "Watch out, Dave!" he called. "They're coming behind you—from the tree!"

Now the company was completely cut off. The twisting creatures were dropping down behind them, sliding through the branches and falling on top of their victims. Josh caught one right across the neck just before the creature had Sarah in its writhing arms.

Miraculously, no one had been bitten. Yet they were at the end of their rope now, huddled together inside a ring of hissing Snakepeople.

Josh began to believe this might be the end. Yet

worse than the thought of death was the knowledge that, with them, died all hope of a new world.

Then for no reason that he could see, every Snake-creature froze like a statue carved out of marble. They looked like a movie stopped in a single frame.

Josh stared at the venomous face of the nearest creature and saw that a film had covered its eyes. It began to sway faintly from side to side.

"What's wrong with them?" he whispered to Sarah.

"Listen!" Sarah said and cocked her head to one side.

Josh heard nothing for a moment. Then a faint, thin melody reached his ears. As the notes grew stronger and stronger, Josh recognized the tones of some kind of flute. Suddenly, out of the trees just to the left of Volka, stepped a man.

He looked like the picture from a story Josh had loved —"The Pied Piper of Hamelin." The stranger wore a peaked green cap with a feather, a short tunic, and brown leather boots. He carried a bow over his shoulder and a sword at his side, but it was the pipe that Josh looked at.

The little instrument was silver with many stops. The melody the stranger played was like none Josh had heard. It almost made him feel drowsy, in spite of the danger.

The strange figure took the pipe from his lips. He looked at the Snakepeople, who were all glassy-eyed and swaying from side to side. Then he said, "They won't be able to do much for about half an hour. However, I think it might be wise to move on a bit."

He had a brown face, very white teeth, and bright black eyes.

"My name is Hamar," he said, "but you'd better introduce yourselves later."

He walked away, and they followed as quickly as they could.

Josh shuddered as he wiped his soiled sword blade on the grass. Killing anything was not to his liking.

They hurried through the forest until finally Hamar drew up.

Then he spoke. "They won't follow us this far. They never come this far away from their pit."

"How do you know?" Mat asked suspiciously.

"I study them." Hamar smiled. "Actually I study biology, but I became interested in these life-forms on my own, so I'm collecting material about them." He nodded with a smile, then added, "They almost had you, didn't they? One bite and it's good-bye to this world."

"Well, you sure saved our bacon," Dave said. He stepped forward and shook Hamar's hand. "I hope there aren't any more of them ahead."

"You're headed that way?" Hamar pointed with his flute. "Well, I'm afraid that country is the worst of all—the Snakepeople, I mean. That place where you are going is crawling with them. I'd think twice before I'd go through there alone."

Hamar's voice sounded grim, and Josh looked ahead fearfully.

"How did you stop them?" Sarah asked.

"There was once something called a *fakir* in Old-world, a kind of snake charmer," Hamar explained. "Well, this new life-form that emerged from the ashes of the Terror—no one knows if they're animal or vegetable. After studying them, I developed the theory that they could be stopped by music. That's what brought me out here in the middle of Serpentland—scientific hunting. That takes care of *my* story. Now, what are you doing here?"

Dave opened his mouth, but before he could speak, Josh broke in. "Oh, just some travelers who lost our way. We're trying to get to the Great Road."

"Well, I can take you there," Hamar volunteered. "It's where I was going anyway. I know where these creatures have their pits, and we can go around them. Wouldn't do to fall in a snakepit."

Josh shuddered at the thought.

"That'll be great," Dave said. "Come on, everybody, let's get out of here."

He hurried them into some sort of order and then walked ahead, talking to Hamar as the rest followed raggedly.

The company walked for two hours, and then Josh saw that they would have to camp out for the night. Hamar led them to an excellent site with good water and cover. After a hearty meal, they sat around the fire and talked.

But they spoke only of the food until after Hamar got up and said, "I'll take a look around. Should be safe, but in this part of the woods you never know."

He left as silently as an Indian, and they began to discuss him.

"I don't trust him," Mat said flatly. "It's just too convenient—his being there at just the right time."

"Oh, Mat, you're too suspicious." Dave grinned at him from across the fire. He pressed his point. "It's the break of a lifetime! Hamar saved us, didn't he? And he can get us to the road. That's all we need. I talked to him all afternoon, and I say he's all right. I think we ought to tell him about our quest."

"No!" Crusoe sat up and spoke in a stronger voice than Josh had heard him use since the beating he had taken.

"Let him guide us to the road if you must. But say nothing to him—or anyone else—if you want to live."

The effort seemed to exhaust Crusoe, and he lay back weakly.

"I agree," Josh chimed in quickly. "He may be all right, but we don't know much about him."

Dave looked at Josh with contempt. "Josh, you're going to have to get over being afraid of everything that moves." He turned to the others and said, "I believe we need help. We know Hamar is strong, and he's smart. Let's tell him our story. He's an adult, and he knows this country like the back of his hand."

"No," Josh objected angrily.

"And I say yes!" Dave retorted.

He got up and started to call Hamar to the fire. But before he could, Josh did something he had never done in his life. He drew back his fist and hit the older boy in the face.

To his surprise, Dave went down. However, Josh's victory was short-lived. Dave immediately jumped up and, with his superior size and skill, began to administer a thorough beating to Josh.

One of Josh's eyes was already closed, and he was bleeding from the nose when Volka stepped in. With a hard hand, he picked up Dave, then set him on the ground at a distance away.

To give Dave credit, when he saw the mess he had made of the smaller boy's face he seemed to feel ashamed. "Oh, Josh, I'm sorry! I have such a rotten temper! Here, take this handkerchief and wipe your face off." He looked around. "I guess I get so carried away I forget to consider what others think. Well, here comes Hamar."

They all sat down as Hamar rejoined them.

If the piper noticed Josh's face, he did not mention it. "Everything seems quiet," Hamar reported. "Have you decided what to do tomorrow?"

They all looked at Josh, who was having trouble breathing through his nose. "I guess Dave is right," he said in a muffled voice. "If you could take us to the road, we'd be mighty grateful."

"No trouble at all," Hamar said. "We should be there before noon."

They all breathed sighs of relief, but for a long time Josh lay awake. He was thinking about the strange figure of Goél. In addition, he felt humiliated at the sorry showing he had made in the fight with Dave. It brought back bitter memories of the failures he had always suffered. The newfound confidence that had been building up in him toppled and fell. He wished he were safely at home again.

Then he realized that home was gone forever. Any home he found would have to be here in this frightening place.

9
Captured!

Breakfast the next morning was a rather sorry affair. Josh was sullen. He refused to eat or even speak to anyone.

True enough, it was raining, and cooking was impossible. But when Dave made an effort to patch up their quarrel by handing Josh a piece of cold meat between two soggy crackers, all Josh did was grunt and draw his coat closer around him.

"Better try to eat a little, Josh," Dave urged. "Looks like it's going to rain all day. You may not get a hot meal for a while."

"I'll eat when I want to!" Josh said mulishly. He knew he was behaving like a child, but he couldn't help it. Things had been going so well until Dave showed up!

They were all sitting around what was left of the campfire when a strange thing happened. Dave and Hamar were talking about how far it was to the road, when Sarah —she would later tell Josh—began to feel most peculiar.

Suddenly she tossed the last bite of cold meat aside, thinking that she was going to be sick. Her head was spinning a little, and the talk of her friends seemed to fade into the distance. She heard the sound of her own voice, and yet she did not understand what she was saying. It was as if she were listening to someone else, but she knew the words were coming from her own lips.

Then she felt the pressure fade, and the world came back. Looking around, Sarah saw that the others were looking at her strangely.

"What's wrong?" she asked shakily.

No one answered for a moment.

Then Dave said, "What was all that stuff you were saying, Sarah? I couldn't understand a word of it."

"I don't know what you're talking about," Sarah said quickly.

"Didn't you understand what you said, Sarah?" Crusoe asked.

"No."

"You were speaking the dialect of Nuworld." He waved his hand at Mat and Volka.

"We all speak it well—but you never learned."

"But how can I speak it if I don't know it?" Sarah cried. "And what did I say?"

"I don't know the answer to the first—except that some strange things are beginning to happen. But you said, 'The way ahead will be dangerous and filled with snares, but he that turns back from the trodden road goes to his own destruction.'"

They were quiet for a moment trying to take it in.

Then Dave spoke briskly. "Well, I don't know about all that jabber, but I do know we've got to get started. It's a long way to the road."

They broke camp quickly, concealing their fears as best they could. Soon they were trooping after Dave and Hamar toward the south.

They could only have gone a few miles when a horse approached from behind. They dived into the bushes, scarcely getting out of sight before a troop of scarlet-clad priests rode by at a full gallop. Josh noticed that the priests were carefully scanning the forest on each side, as if looking for something.

"Whew!" Dave said as they returned to the road. "That was close! Everyone look sharp. There may be more of them."

No other patrols appeared at once, but after about an hour, Sarah called out, "Crusoe! What's the matter?"

She knelt beside the old man, who had slumped to the ground. Crusoe's face was pale, and his breathing was uneven. He tried to say something but failed. Then his head sank forward on his breast.

"We've got to get him off the road," Sarah said.

"Right!" Dave agreed. "Volka, will you take him over to that clump of bushes? We can rest there until he's better."

"Don't—think he's going—to get—better," a voice said haltingly.

Sarah turned to see Mat weaving in an alarming fashion. Then Mat too began to sag dangerously.

Josh and Dave grabbed him and helped him to the small grove where Sarah had opened a canteen and was trying to give Crusoe a drink.

"He's unconscious!" she said in a whisper. "What can we do?"

"Listen," Josh said suddenly. There was the sound of traffic on the road again—men walking and riding.

"Everyone keep still," Dave whispered.

Josh peered through the bushes and saw a band of men dressed in black uniforms. They wore the strange device of the Sanhedrin on their chests.

He groaned. "Oh, no!"

"What's the matter?" Sarah asked.

"They've stopped to rest!" he hissed. "Keep quiet, everyone!"

Sure enough, the troop had halted and began to sit down not thirty feet from where the little band huddled. Josh clearly heard the sound of a cork being pulled from a bottle and then a coarse voice saying, "How much longer we got to keep this up? My feet are killing me!"

"You'll keep walking as long as the Chief Interrogator

tells you to!" another voice, evidently that of the first speaker's superior, answered. "You ain't no tireder than the rest of us."

"Well, there ain't no sense to it," the first insisted. He apparently took a long pull at his bottle. "Ain't likely them Sleepers will be out in plain sight just askin' to be caught."

At the word "Sleepers," Josh glanced wildly at Sarah. He saw that she was as pale as he felt.

"Ah," the second voice went on, "but there's the reward, don't forget."

"Sure, I've not forgotten that," said the first. "And how much did you say it was?"

"One thousand in gold!"

"Ah, now, there's a sum a man could do a bit with! But I still say they won't be on the road."

"You ain't a sergeant, but if you *was*, you'd know that it don't much matter where we are. Whoever sees them will hear about that reward, and they got to tell *somebody*. So if we gets told, we finds 'em."

"But then *they* gets the reward!"

"Oh, no, they don't. We'll see that they get a nice letter from the government, and *we'll* handle the cash."

They all laughed loudly and began boasting about what they would do with the gold.

"But are you sure that folks know about the reward?" someone asked.

"How could they not know about it when the Chief Interrogator has had a notice posted in every village within two hundred miles? Oh, they'll be seen all right enough!"

The soldiers rested only ten minutes, but it seemed like days before the helpless band heard the sergeant order his men down the road.

They waited until they could no longer hear the troops. Then they all heaved deep sighs of relief.

"I thought sure they had us," Volka said.

Josh saw that Volka's hands were not steady, and he was a little less ashamed of his own shakiness.

"What do we do *now*?" Sarah asked. "Even if we were all well, it would be hard enough to travel without being seen, but Crusoe and Mat are getting worse."

There was a silence, and they all looked at Dave.

Dave spoke hurriedly, "Well . . . I suppose . . ." He paused uncertainly, then must have got a glimpse of Josh's grin. He seemed to make a decision. "I'd *like* to go on, of course, but that's impossible now. We'll have to go back."

"Go back where?" Josh asked sharply.

If Josh had been older and wiser, he would have realized that his attitude was simply helping Dave reinforce his rash decision—a decision Josh didn't like one bit. But all that struck Josh at the moment was that Dave wanted to give up.

"We'll go back to the cave." Dave's answers came smoothly now. "We'll be safe there. There's plenty of food and water, and there'll be time for the patrols to get tired . . ."

He talked faster as if trying to convince himself, but he refused to meet Sarah's eye.

"Well, let's get started," Hamar quietly prompted.

And they would have pushed on had it not been for Volka. The group had looked to him for physical help, but no one had really considered that he could make any other kind of contribution. So it came as a shock when they heard him ask, "Well, what about that thing Sarah said this morning?"

"What about it?" Dave said sharply.

Josh could have hugged the giant! "That's right, Dave. We're not supposed to turn back, no matter what!"

Dave's face grew red. He seemed to turn fiery whenever someone questioned anything he said or did. "That isn't important," he snapped. "We didn't even understand the words, so they can't have any meaning."

"Why not?" Sarah asked quietly. She was looking at Dave with a different light in her eyes, as if she were seeing something for the first time.

"In the first place," Dave argued, "it's impossible to go on. There are patrols everywhere, and we've got two sick men. We would go on if we could, but there are some things that just can't be done."

They all tried to talk at once, and the argument grew louder until a new voice broke through.

"Would you mind if I say a word?" The travelers looked around, startled. For a moment, they had forgotten that there was a relative stranger in their midst. Hamar was sitting off to one side. He spoke with a small smile on his face. "I've tried not to notice who you are —but it's getting a little difficult."

Dave broke in suddenly. "I told Hamar last night who we are. He's anxious to help us."

Dave must have read the look of betrayal on the faces around him. Dave had heard, as they all had, Crusoe's instructions to keep their identity a secret. Dave hurried on before they could accuse him. "Oh, it's all right. Hamar figured out who we were anyway. And he's with us all the way. I mean, he's no friend to the Sanhedrin. Isn't that right, Hamar?"

Hamar smoothly reassured them. "Well, there's no reason for any of you to believe me, but Dave is right. I've always been sort of a rebel, and I saw at once that you were hiding from the priests. So if you want to trust me, maybe I can help you. If not, I'll just be moving on."

He got to his feet, but before he could move, Josh called out.

"Hold him, Volka." The giant's massive hand closed firmly on Hamar's neck.

"Well" —Hamar actually smiled— "I see your point.

It wouldn't do to turn me loose if I wanted the reward, would it?"

If Hamar had been angry, or if he had attempted to get away, quite likely Volka would have wrung his neck. However, he was so quiet and had such a relaxed look on his face that Josh had the feeling that he was on their side.

"Actually," said Hamar, "if you would like to go on —instead of going back, that is—I can show you a way."

"Do you trust him, Sarah?" Josh asked.

Sarah looked carefully into Hamar's face.

Then she nodded slowly. "Yes, I think I do. What else can we do?"

Hamar looked at her with a gentle smile. "Yes, at times we must trust someone—even if they fail us, perhaps?"

Then he looked at the others. "What is it to be?"

Dave nodded quickly, then Volka.

Slowly Josh nodded his agreement also.

"It's not an easy way," Hamar said firmly, removing Volka's hand from his neck. "We'll have to carry this gentleman." He indicated Crusoe.

Volka gently picked up the unconscious hunchback. The others agreed to help Mat. Hamar got them all up, and soon the travelers were moving slowly down the road.

They had gone less than a mile when Hamar led them off onto a path. It was a detour that Josh had not noticed.

"Where does this go?" Dave asked.

"It will take us to the Great Road. We follow it until we come to Roaring Horse—that's a river—and then we follow the river until we come to the Great Road."

"How long will it take?" Josh asked.

"Two days usually. With sick men, maybe three. We'll camp at the river tonight and go on tomorrow."

It was a difficult trip to the river. Rain was still falling lightly, and the path was overgrown with vines and tangles of thorns.

Fortunately, Mat grew better and was able to walk as they went slowly along. Volka easily managed the weight of Crusoe, so the group progressed steadily through the dense forest.

Hamar seemed to know every tree. He even pointed out some of the strange vegetation and rare animals that thrived in the woods.

Finally they reached Roaring Horse River, a wide, swift-flowing stream with wild-breaking whitecaps. Quickly Hamar set up camp, and soon everyone was sitting around the fire, eating steaks from a small antelope that the piper had brought down.

The fire burned cheerfully in the darkness, and there was a strange new sense of safety that all of them seemed to feel. Crusoe had begun to stir, and Sarah made him some broth that he tasted, then gulped down.

Hamar walked over to the old man and knelt beside him, looking him full in the face. After a moment's silence, he said, "Sir, you are right not to trust strangers. I will hope to show you that I am not dangerous."

For a long time Crusoe looked at the strange figure. Then he smiled, nodded slightly, and whispered in a weak voice, "We shall see."

Josh felt much easier now that that hurdle was over. He slept like a rock that night, but by the cold light of morning the safety he had felt in the warmth of the fire had faded.

The company gathered their gear and plunged through the overgrowth beside the river. It was not long before they began to ascend a steep incline. Soon most of them were panting for breath.

"It gets steeper from here on," Hamar shouted. He had to speak loudly because the river was growing more narrow, and the water was beginning to roar.

Looking ahead, Josh saw that the river disappeared

into a deep canyon. Their group was poised on one lip of the abyss.

As they moved ahead, the trees grew scarce. The bushes and vegetation thinned out. There was no doubt now—they were climbing a mountain along the narrow path cut into its steep side. The ledge was at least six feet wide, but the wall of the canyon rose sharply on their left. On the right, far down—so far that it made Josh dizzy just to peer over the edge—the roar of the river increased.

"Why do they call this Roaring Horse River?" Sarah asked Hamar.

"Once in a while, horses lose their footing in the stream and are pulled into the rapids and through the canyon. When that happens, they—well, they roar!" He shook his head sadly. "It isn't a pleasant sound, I can assure you."

"Are they all killed?" Sarah asked, peering at the wild whitecaps raging far below.

"Oh, yes, nothing could live in that turmoil," Hamar said, waving a hand toward the river. Then he stood up saying, "Not too far to go now. Here, let me play a tune to cheer you."

He pulled his silver flute from his knapsack and raised it to his lips.

"Won't somebody hear us?" Sarah asked nervously.

Hamar looked at her in amusement, then waved his flute at the sky. "A bird, perhaps?" He laughed. Then he began to pipe a merry little tune as the group marched down the narrow path.

Soon they were approaching what appeared to be a ledge of stone. Josh felt that it must be the very crest of the mountain path. He started forward more quickly, but suddenly there was a movement. The little party stopped as suddenly as if they had run into a wall.

A priest clad in scarlet with a gold insignia on his chest was barring their way, a cruel smile on his pale face.

"I arrest you all in the name of the High Priest of the Sanhedrin."

"Run! Back down the mountain!" Josh called. He started to run but had not gone ten feet when four red-robed priests slipped down from the rocks overhead and barred his path.

"Pull back," Josh shouted as he drew his sword. "Get Mat and Crusoe behind us. We'll make our stand there!"

There was a little hollow in the side of the mountain, and they gathered there, placing Mat and Crusoe inside the hollow. But their situation was hopeless. The soldier-priests had drawn bows, and cruel arrows with steel tips were trained on them all.

"Drop your weapons," the leader commanded sternly. "You will die here if you resist."

He began advancing and was joined by five other soldiers. The troopers coming up the path moved forward and began to squeeze the little group as in a vise.

"We're trapped," Dave cried and threw down his sword with a bitter cry.

Slowly Volka dropped his weapon, then Mat and Sarah did the same.

Now, according to all reason, Josh should have done so, but he was filled with an anger he had never known. He gripped his sword fiercely and stepped out on a rock that projected over the roaring river. He turned to meet the approach of the sinister soldiers.

"If you will throw down your weapon," the priest said, "you will have a fair inquisition. If you are not one of the—Sleepers." His lips curled as he spat out the word. "You will only have a term in prison for defying the Sanhedrin. Throw down the sword."

Light glinted on the arrows of the soldiers, and Josh heard someone begging him to surrender. He thought it was Sarah, but he could not be sure because something was happening to his hearing.

Even the loud roaring of the river was growing fainter. He stood on the rock over the raging water with arrows trained on his heart. But suddenly he was not afraid, for he could not hear the river or the voice of the priest telling him to surrender. Instead, he heard the still, strong voice that he had heard once before. The voice was giving him a command.

He shook his head as if to clear it, then he whispered, "Is—is that *you*, Goél?"

And the answer came. *"Yes, I am here."*

Without hesitation Josh said, "What would you have me to do, Sire?"

"Do you believe in me, Joshua?"

"Yes! Yes, I believe in you. I don't know who you are, but I believe in you!"

"Would you do anything I commanded you to do?"

Josh answered instantly. "Yes! Anything, Goél!"

There was a moment's pause. Then Josh heard the voice say calmly but with authority, *"I command you to throw yourself into the river, Joshua."*

If Josh had had time to think, he could have found plenty of reasons for not doing what the voice commanded. Even as he stood there, still another voice began nagging at his mind, whispering, *"But who is Goél? He may be evil."*

The second voice grew stronger—so strong that Josh knew that if he listened any longer, he would not be able to obey Goél's command. So without a moment's further hesitation, he threw his sword high into the air and cried out in a piercing voice.

Then he flung himself off the rock and plunged down, down, down until he disappeared into the murky depths of the waters.

10

In the Tower

Sarah never forgot the sickening feeling that swept over her as she watched Josh disappear into the froth of the churning river. A scream rose in her throat, but she did not have time to make a sound. The iron hand of one of the priests closed on her arm. She was dragged down the steep path along with the other travelers.

"He'll be one less to worry about," said one of the swarthy guards, grinning at her. "By the time the Questioning is over, you'll be wishing you had gone into the drink with him."

"Be silent!" the head priest commanded. One look of his burning eye was enough to turn the guard's dark face pale ivory.

The trip to the Tower was long, and Sarah was reeling with aching legs by the time they passed through the heavy stone wall.

"Put them in the Common until the Questioning is ordered," the tall priest commanded.

The prisoners were pushed down a dark, moldy corridor of massive stones until they passed through a large court. Sarah thought she heard strange snorting noises, but in the darkness she could see nothing.

Using two keys, the guard opened a huge steel door. Without ceremony, the prisoners were shoved through, and the heavy door clanged shut behind them.

Two or three torches flickered in the gloom. When Sarah's eyes grew accustomed to the prison, she gave a frightened cry. "Oh—oh, Mr. Crusoe," she whispered, and then her voice choked with fright. The little band was surrounded by ominous dark forms moving in the shadows of the torchlight.

Suddenly a familiar voice called, "Hey, Sarah!" Out of darkness stepped Jake, his face alight with pleasure at seeing them.

"Jake!" Sarah said, running to hug him. "We thought you were dead!"

"Are you all right? Did they hurt you?" Dave asked.

"Well—" the little redhead grinned "—those Questionings aren't much like exams back in school, but they haven't hurt me—yet. Tam is OK too. He's being questioned now, but he ought to be back. Hey, what's wrong with Crusoe?"

Crusoe had suddenly collapsed on the stone floor.

"Here," Hamar said quickly, "he's fainted. We'd better try to get him warmed up."

Hamar looked at the dark forms around the room and said something in a strange language. There was a rustle in the shadows, and some of the creatures began to edge toward them.

This time Sarah did not scream, but she took Dave's hand and realized that he was trembling too.

"Who *are* they?" he whispered.

"What?" Hamar asked, looking around. "Oh, you haven't been inside the Tower before, have you? Well, these are some of the enemies of the Sanhedrin. Don't be afraid. They won't harm you. They're prisoners too."

As he spoke, two prisoners came forward and said something to Hamar in the tongue he had used. Then they picked up Crusoe and moved him toward another area.

"Hey!" Jake objected. "Where are they taking him?"

"They've a warm bed and some food, and that's what he needs."

Sure enough, as the young people watched, the two

prisoners were joined by several others. They placed the limp body of the old man on a rough wooden bunk and wrapped him with warm blankets. One of them began to chafe his hands and another his feet. In a few moments, Crusoe's eyes flickered open. Then one of the prisoners produced a bowl of some kind of soup.

Hamar said, "I think he'll be all right. You watch him. I want to see if I can get one of the guards to come to the door."

When Hamar disappeared into the gloom, the group around the three young people began to draw in closer. There were about six of the strangers.

The one feeding the soup to Crusoe was the most frightening. He had a dwarfish body that looked as if it had been driven into a large lump with a huge mallet. His head was shapeless. A drooling mouth, a potato nose, and wicked little eyes under beetling brows stood out of the lumpy mass.

Beside him there was a pair of Gemini twins—small females with long black hair and fair skin. Nothing frightening about them.

But the three strange creatures standing near the twins were like nothing Sarah had seen before. They were all small boned and very thin. They looked like athletes, runners perhaps. It was not their bodies, but something else that made Sarah draw closer to Jake and Dave.

"They're *awful!*" she whispered.

All three of the strange creatures had normal, rather attractive faces, except that each had one terribly disproportionate feature. One had huge eyes. In the darkness, they looked like twin mirrors.

Another had ears like those of an elephant. Even as Sarah whispered, one ear twitched in the direction of her voice, while the other independently swept the room like a radar antenna.

The third creature had a nose that extended at least six inches in front of his face. It twitched and moved like a piece of soft rubber tubing as he sniffed and snorted.

"We look stranger all the time, don't we?" Jake said with a crooked grin.

It did Sarah good to see the tough little redhead able to smile in such a dark place.

"Ah, you speak Oldworld!" said one of the strange creatures.

The travelers turned with a start toward the ugly gnome who had finished feeding Crusoe. The little man was smiling at them.

"What did you say?" asked Sarah nervously.

"You speak Oldworld talk," he repeated and wrapped another blanket about Crusoe. Then he turned to them again. "Not so many people speak Oldworld anymore."

His voice was very nice, much like that of a radio announcer. Now Sarah saw that the gleam in his eyes was not evil at all—just bright and intelligent.

"Please, Mr. . . ." Sarah paused helplessly.

The gnome said, "My name Kybus."

Solemnly, first Sarah, then Dave, and finally Jake shook the little gnome's hand.

"Well, Kybus, who are these people?" Dave asked, motioning to the three prisoners with the outsized features.

"They? Oh, you never seen Hunter before?"

"Which one is the hunter?" Jake asked.

"*They* is Hunter!" Kybus insisted with a nod. "All three is Hunter. They get after *anything*—they catch him! See, smell, hear—they get him."

One of the pretty Gemini twins said something in a language filled with R's.

Kybus turned to them, and for a long moment he seemed to be weighing something in his mind. Finally he shrugged his shoulders and said, "Are you in the House?"

The three young people looked at each other in be-wilderment.

"What house?" Sarah asked.

Kybus looked at them, but did not answer. Finally he said, "You better eat, rest now."

Then the young people began to eat some of the broth that Crusoe had been fed. When they finished, they went to sleep so suddenly it was almost comical. Jake fell into a doze in the middle of a sentence, and Sarah was limp with exhaustion.

They had no way of measuring time, but when Sarah awoke she felt that she had slept the clock around.

"Jake? Dave?" she called.

"They still asleep," a voice said.

Sarah sat up to see Kybus standing beside Crusoe, who was sitting up in bed.

"Oh, Mr. Crusoe, you're better!" she cried. She ran to his side and took his hands.

"For now I am, thanks to our friend here." Crusoe nodded at Kybus. "Are you all right?" he asked Sarah.

"Well—yes, but—oh, Mr. Crusoe, poor Josh!"

She began to weep.

Crusoe did not answer, but she felt his frail hands stroking her hair.

Their voices had awakened the others. Immediately Jake and Dave, with Mat close at their sides, drew around them in a circle.

Jake began questioning almost at once. "Say, what's this 'house' they keep talking about? And why are we here?"

Crusoe held up his hand. "My boy, Kybus here can tell you about the House. It's the reason he and all the others are in this place." He paused, and they looked at him expectantly.

The gnome softly cleared his throat and spoke. "Everywhere in Nuworld, there is people who believe that One is coming. Yes, One is coming. And He is building House."

Kybus fell into a speech pattern that Sarah seemed to recognize but couldn't quite place. It was flowing, and it rose in intensity from time to time.

Finally Sarah recognized what it was. "He's *preaching*!" she whispered.

The others nodded, for they had all heard this cadence from certain intense preachers and rabbis on religious occasions. Kybus was saying that a Deliverer would come and make the world good again. Evil would be eliminated, and justice would flow back into the world.

"Sounds like a prophet," Jake murmured.

Finally Kybus drew to a close. Yet, his last line astonished Sarah more than anything he had said before. He gravely announced, "The Deliverer will come—when the Seven Sleepers wake!"

"What!" Dave exclaimed. He looked at the others with wild eyes.

"Do you think—" Sarah began.

"I'll be a—" Jake began.

Suddenly there was a clanging sound as the gate closed. Soon two guards appeared and threw a limp body down at their feet.

"The girl," one of the guards commanded, nodding at Sarah.

They reached for Sarah, but before they could drag her off, Crusoe put his hands on her head, and Sarah heard him saying something. She could not understand the words, but as he spoke, a warm sense of security suddenly filled her. She drew back and looked with wide eyes at the old man. "Thank you, Mr. Crusoe. I'll be all right now."

She turned and walked quietly away with the guards.

"Well, I'll say this," Jake said in quiet amazement as they left, "she has got courage!"

"She has more than that," Crusoe said softly.

The voices of her friends faded into the distance as Sarah calmly followed the guard. She was in such a strange state. She knew she should be frightened, but she had no fear at all—just a strange sense of being watched and loved.

Her captors led her into a room where six red-cloaked men sat at a long table. Yet even at the sight of the menacing strangers, Sarah's serenity held. She felt that she was somehow outside herself, looking on. She saw herself pushed into a hard chair. Then she saw one of the hooded priests nod.

From the darkness along the wall, a frightening figure wearing a cloak with mystic symbols began to make weird gestures and mutter garbled phrases. There was a sense of evil in the room. Sarah knew that if she had not been wrapped in some sort of protective spell, she would have been totally at the mercy of this sorcerer.

"Well, is she ready?" Elmas asked, for it was he indeed.

"I—I cannot say. There is something interfering with the spell."

"If you are too incompetent to deal with a small child, perhaps we need a new sorcerer!"

"No! She is ready!" the sorcerer said quickly.

"Very well. Begin the Questioning," Elmas commanded.

And then Sarah felt very strange. The sorcerer and the six red-robed men began to shoot tortuous questions at her.

"Who are you? Where do you come from?" they demanded.

Even in her strange state, Sarah knew that if these men found out who she was, it would be death to all her companions. Just as she began to give way a little before the questioners, a sudden knowledge invaded her. It was more striking than a spoken voice, for she seemed not to hear it with her ears alone but with her whole body.

"Do not be afraid. I will help you to answer all questions," the voice assured her.

So it was that Sarah heard herself responding, but she knew that she was not controlling her words.

Finally Elmas said, "Enough! Bring in the old man. There is nothing in this one."

As she went toward the door, Sarah heard someone mutter, "This Uprising is getting out of hand."

"Uprising!" Elmas snarled furiously. "When I am through, there will be no Uprising—if there ever has been. I think it is a tale made up by children and idiots!"

"Very likely, my lord," another said smoothly. "And what shall we do with these prisoners?"

"Split them up," Elmas ordered roughly. "All of them to different work camps. Let them serve in the mines. They will not be able to follow their so-called deliverer if they're worked to death!"

11

The Visitation of Goél

For the three days following Sarah's Questioning, the group waited fearfully to be dragged off to the mines. During that time Crusoe would have died had it not been for the kindness of the Nuworld prisoners. One by one, the travelers were taken for interrogation. Yet, each time, those who remained in the cell seemed to protect the one being questioned with their thoughts.

"You know," Jake mused, "I think there must be something to this." He looked a little embarrassed but continued. "I mean, when I go to the Questioning, it's —it's like it isn't even me."

"I know what you mean." Dave nodded. Then his face grew very sober. "But this can't go on long. We've got to get out of here."

"But, Dave, how?" Sarah asked.

"I don't know how, Sarah, but you were the one who heard what Elmas said. We'll all wind up deep in the mines if we don't get out of here." He rose and said, "Let's go talk to the rest of them about escaping."

"Maybe we shouldn't tell everyone." Sarah suggested. "Let's ask Crusoe. I—I wish Josh were here."

"Sure, Sarah," Dave said, "but he's not, so we'll just have to do the best we can."

They waited until later that night to talk to their fellow travelers, for during the afternoon Tam was brought in. As expected, Mat attempted to make little of seeing his twin.

111

"Well," Mat grunted, "about time you turned up. Probably been having a good time for yourself while we've been sitting in this hole!"

"Ho!" shouted Tam. "*You're* the one who's been living it up!"

"Me! What do you mean?"

"Why, look at these two young ladies you've been romancing." Tam pointed delightedly at the Gemini twins, Rama and Amar.

The twins giggled suddenly at Mat's discomfort, but before Tam could push the matter, Hamar dropped a bombshell.

"I hate to be the bearer of ill tidings," he said, "but I'm afraid our time is about up. I've been making friends with the guard that comes on night duty—bribing him, actually. He says the word is out that tomorrow we'll be shipped out of here."

A dread fell on Sarah and apparently on all the others as well.

"Them mines," Kybus said heavily, "they no good."

"Like I've been saying," Dave said, "we've got to get out of here. Let's find out what Crusoe says."

They found Crusoe and Volka sitting in a quiet corner of the common prison.

"Mr. Crusoe," Dave began, "we have to get out of here—now! They're sending us to the mines tomorrow."

"Dave's right," Sarah seconded. "And we'll die there and never see each other again."

They all began talking about escape until Hamar interrupted. "I don't think there's any way out," he remarked grimly. "You know that court out there? Well, I don't know exactly what's out there at night, but whatever it is, it's pretty bad. The guard won't even talk about it, and he's a pretty tough fellow."

"Are you saying we shouldn't do anything?" Jake demanded.

"Not at all. I'm saying I don't see how we can get out. It's not possible."

An argument broke out, but Crusoe said nothing until they had worn themselves out. Finally, in his old quiet voice he spoke. "I have no word on this. I can't say what to do, but I think we'd better just wait until there is a word."

"Mr. Crusoe," Dave said hastily, "I know you believe in that business—and I do too. But we've been given common sense. Mine tells me we'd better try to break out of here."

Crusoe looked at Dave peculiarly. Finally he said, "My son, without a hand to lead you, how could you find your way?"

Dave looked shamefaced, and they finally broke up, some to eat, some to sleep fitfully.

Sarah was confused. "I don't know what to think," she said to Jake. "Mr. Crusoe is so wise—but it's getting to be so *close*."

She finally lay down on the hard bunk and closed her eyes. Her head was swimming, and for a long time she tried to sleep. Just when she was about to slip off, she heard a voice call her name.

"Sarah."

"Yes?" she answered sleepily.

"Awake, Sarah."

The voice came so clearly that she sat straight up on her bunk. There, not five feet away was a stranger in a dark robe that had been cut from very rough cloth.

"Who—who are you?" she whispered faintly. It was so odd—she was afraid, yet at the same time she had never felt more safe in her whole life. She had seen him before —or heard him!

113

"If I tell you my name," the strange figure said, "it will mean that you will have to make a choice. And the choice may be hard. Do you want to know?"

Slowly Sarah nodded. "Yes, I want very much to know you."

"Ah, that is even more serious." The man smiled, and his strong face was both sad and joyful at once. "Many want to know my name that they may use it for their own ends. But they do not know me."

"I want to know you, please," Sarah whispered.

Sarah had been taught not to trust strangers. But this man, though a complete stranger, was somehow different. He was not handsome. In fact, his face was rather plain. But his eyes . . ! Sarah was unable to look away from them.

Dark, with light flecks near the pupil, they seemed to have a warmth that crossed the short distance that lay between them. In his glance, she felt the same sense of safety she had felt during the Questioning.

"You can call me Goél," he said. "That is one of my names. Later you will know others."

"Yes, Goél," Sarah whispered.

He smiled at her briefly then grew serious. "Daughter, tomorrow they plan to take you from this place to die alone in the mines."

"Oh, Goél!" Sarah said fearfully. She reached out her hand to him as she had to her father when she was very small.

He took her hand and held it firmly. "You must believe in what I tell you, Sarah. It is not my purpose for you to go to the mines. I have come to open a door for you."

"And for all of us?" Sarah asked quickly.

"Yes, for all of you, all of you who will believe."

"Oh, Goél, come with me now, and you can tell them all about it."

She rose, but he pulled her back and said carefully, "Sarah, I will open the door. Do you believe me?"

"Oh, Goél, yes, I believe you!"

"But you must go to the door without me."

She drooped at this.

"If you will believe in me strongly enough, you will not fail. Wake up all your friends and tell them what you have seen. Tell them about me. And tell them that you have my word that tonight I will set the prisoners free. Can you do that, Sarah?"

"But . . ." She searched wildly for an excuse. "They'll never believe me."

He did not answer, nor did he smile anymore. He fixed his eyes on her face and waited. Finally he said, "I cannot help you to convince them. I will open the door, but you have to believe enough to get to that door. Goodbye, Sarah. I'll be waiting for you on the other side of the door."

How he left, Sarah could not exactly say. He was there, then he was not there, and she was rubbing her eyes hard.

"Goél!" she cried out, then louder, "Goél!"

"What is it, Sarah?" Dave called.

She saw that Dave and Jake, who had been dozing close by, had been awakened by her call. Then the rest of the prisoners began to stir and gather around her.

"Are you all right, child?" Crusoe asked. "I heard you call out, and I was afraid for you. Who did you call?"

Crusoe's question put Sarah in a very awkward position. It's one thing to have a dream and another to tell it before a crowd, no matter how close they are. The hardest thing of all is to convince them that your dream really wasn't a dream at all.

Sarah struggled awkwardly until Dave said kindly, "Oh, she just had a bad dream."

"No!" Sarah said quickly. "It wasn't a bad dream. It was something else. Mr. Crusoe, did you ever hear of someone named—Goél?"

Crusoe straightened up and looked directly at her. "Goél! What do you know about Goél?"

"Well, he was here tonight."

"Here?" Dave questioned. "What do you mean, here? Where is he?"

"I hope you won't laugh—but I was alone in the darkness, and this man named Goél suddenly appeared. He talked to me."

"Oh, come on, Sarah! You just had a nightmare. Look, there's no one here." Dave swept his arm around the large open room.

"Wait a minute, Dave," Crusoe interrupted. "I'd like to hear what you saw, Sarah."

Sarah would have shrugged it off then, for she saw doubt on Dave's face. But with Crusoe's encouragement, she told them what she had seen and heard. "And so we've got to leave here tonight and go to that door," she concluded.

"Well, I don't believe your dreams, but I've been saying that all along," Dave said grumpily. He waved his hand at the courtyard. "We can't even get *through* that door."

"Oh, yes, we can get through that door," Crusoe said matter-of-factly.

"What?" Dave cried with some irritation. "I guess you'll work a little miracle?"

Crusoe shrugged. "Getting out past that door has never been a problem." He smiled. "It's always been possible. But what to do then? If we go out in daylight, the guards will see us. If we go out at night, that thing—whatever it is—is waiting."

"But it's our only chance, isn't it?" Sarah said.

She found a surprising supporter in Mat. "I think it's all hopeless. But if there's only one door, you don't have to like it. You just have to take it."

"I agree, Mat," Crusoe said. He looked at Sarah carefully. "Do you believe this man Goél, Sarah?"

"Yes, I do," she said stiffly but firmly.

"Then you can go first," he answered. He turned to Volka. "Are you ready, friend?"

"Yes."

Sarah and the others followed Volka and Crusoe to the massive steel door and stood looking at the thing.

"Well, how do we open that?" Dave challenged. He was obviously miffed at not being on center stage.

"Oh, Volka can open it, I'm pretty sure," Crusoe said.

Crusoe nodded at Volka.

The giant determinedly wrapped his huge hand around the strap of steel that formed the small window. As easily as a normal man would straighten out wet clay, Volka pulled the steel free, then reached outside. Sarah heard him slide back the heavy bar, and the door swung free.

"Ho! That was easy!" he said cheerfully.

Then Sarah felt every eye on her. She knew that this was the most terrible moment of her life. Every fear she had ever known was laughable compared to her dread of the thing that lurked outside. She did not see how she could ever make herself go through that door into the awful darkness. How cheerful the cell seemed in contrast to what lay outside!

Then Sarah began to hear the voice of doubt. The voice chided her as one who lived by dreams, dreams with a foolish message.

The voice nibbled at her courage, wearing it down, until she heard Dave saying spitefully, "What will you do, Sarah, if you look back and nobody's following you?"

117

Somehow the remark needled Sarah into action. Looking directly into Dave's eyes she declared, "I won't be looking back to see who's following me, Dave."

Then, before she could give way to that nagging fear, she swung the door open and marched confidently into the darkness.

It was so black that she could not see her hand before her face. But she had looked out the door often and knew that the gate that led out of the prison was about fifty yards at the end of the cobblestone walk she felt beneath her feet.

Don't think! Don't run! Just believe in Goél. He's there, right on the other side of that gate.

But was he? The nagging voice began again, suggesting that she had made up the dream herself. Only by saying with each step, "Goél, Goél," did she manage to keep a steady pace.

And then she heard it! She had been hearing the sound of the others following her, but this was something else.

She did not actually see the thing, even though in the darkness the sky itself seemed to be blotted out by a mountainous shape. Nor did she smell it, though suddenly it seemed that the breath of an open grave touched her face. Nor did she really hear it, though a heavy throb like a massive drum or monstrous heartbeat seemed to touch her ears.

No, more than anything else, Sarah simply knew that the *thing* was there beside the path. The darkness grew darker, the smell more deathly, and the throbbing filled the air. She heard the others beginning to moan and realized that they were on the point of panic—and death.

Sarah was no singer. As a matter of fact, she sang off-key. Neither was she a writer or a poet. But at that moment she opened her mouth, and her voice broke sweetly on the dark night air. She began to sing in a strong voice.

> "Goél is my daysman.
> My redeemer and lord is he.
> From all the danger of death
> He has delivered me."

As she sang, the air grew sweeter, the night less dark, and the sound of her voice replaced the monstrous throbbing. Then, with the last of her courage, Sarah reached the outer gate and pushed it. It swung open, and on the other side she fell into the arms of the one who had slipped the lock.

She cried out in joy, "Goél! Goél!"

12

The Fifth Sleeper

In the years that followed, Josh would rarely talk about what happened when he plunged into the depths of Roaring Horse River. Once he tried to tell Sarah.

"Well, it was like I—well, really, it was something like—like dying, I guess, Sarah," he whispered. Then he continued in a stronger voice, "The water was cold—I knew that. Yet, I didn't feel cold.

"And you know those rocks were like knives, but I was never cut once! Sarah, it was like—like I was surrounded by some sort of—oh, I just can't tell you. I don't know."

And he gave up trying to explain.

The moment the cold waters closed over his head, Josh knew he was dead, but just as he began rolling over and over in the powerful current, something happened. He felt himself surrounded by a strange sense of warmth and safety. With one part of his mind he knew he was dying. Yet he felt somehow as he had felt when he was a small child and his father had held him close after a nightmare.

Josh's hopes faded. But just then, a tiny light appeared in the darkness. The light grew stronger, and as it grew, the voice returned again. Josh heard himself joining the song:

"When my soul fainted within me
I remembered Goél,
And my prayer came in unto you,
into your holy temple."

Then Josh seemed to hear the voice of Goél speaking. After that, he came to himself. He was sitting in the still waters on a sand bar.

Josh slowly got up and looked himself over for injuries. To his amazement, he was not even bruised or scratched. Then he looked around. It seemed that the sky was bluer and the grass greener than he had ever seen them.

His hearing seemed sharper too. He could hear a tiny cricket singing from twenty yards away. He began to walk slowly downstream, not knowing where he was or what he was going to do.

His friends were in jail, he had no food, no money. Yet somehow Josh felt good. He actually laughed out loud, then paused, amazed at himself.

He wandered on, totally unafraid. When he came across a path that led away from the river canyon, he took it without hesitation. He soon reached a crest that offered a clear view of the countryside. The first thing he saw was a city.

"That's it!" he said softly, then sat down on a tree stump to think.

"Let's see—what did the song say about the fifth Sleeper? I remember . . .

> *'Close to the stars the Sleeper lies,*
> *atop a tower rising high,*
> *reaching to the windows of the sky.*
>
> *And yet—the waters o'er him flow,*
> *Such watery depths he lies below.'"*

Josh was puzzled by the words of the song, but he truly believed that the city in the distance must be the place where the fifth Sleeper lay. He had quickly figured out that 25 was the first number and 17 the last. Then he found the intersection of those numbers on the map he carried in his mind.

He thought of the words again and murmured his puzzlement. How could the Sleeper be up in a tower and down under the waves at the same time?

For a long time, Josh sat and tried to piece it together. Finally he got up and started toward the city. Before he took the first step, he spoke out loud to no one in particular.

"Well, I don't have Sarah's heart to help me this time." He glanced around self-consciously. "Goél, I'll just have to trust you to get me there."

It was dusk by the time he reached the gates of the city. Once there, he kept himself hidden by dodging behind trees or buildings. Red-robed guards were looking carefully at those who filed through the entrance, and Josh racked his brain trying to figure out a way to get in.

He waited two hours, watching for his chance to slip through unnoticed. The light slowly began to fade, and Josh felt sure that they would soon lock the gates.

Just then he heard the sound of heavy hooves. Peering through the darkness, he saw a train of camels approaching. Later, he would wonder if he had actually heard a voice ordering him to join the caravan or if the thought was his own.

In any case, Josh took the chance without thinking. There were only three or four drivers, and he slipped by them easily, dodging between the shuffling animals.

Once among the herd, Josh lost control. He was pushed and jostled by the smelly beasts, but he suffered no harm and was swept inside the city. As the last animal entered, Josh slunk quickly into a dark alley. He heard the closing of the iron gate.

Rather aimlessly, he stole along the alley until he noticed that the full moon was already lighting up the entire city.

He was getting hungry, but he knew that he would have to find the Sleeper before dawn. So he found a wide street that seemed to go through the city and began to examine the words of the song again.

"Well, one thing is clear," he muttered to himself. "The Sleeper is in a tower. Guess I'll try to find the tower. Then I can worry about the rest."

Finding the tower turned out to be quite simple. The town had been built of adobe houses and other buildings, none of them more than two or three stories high. But beneath the bright face of the full moon a massive tower hung over the city. Josh found his way to the tower in less than an hour.

He felt strangely apprehensive when he finally turned the last corner and came face-to-face with his destination. Strange astrological signs were on the doors, and somehow the place seemed evil.

Josh chose one of the doors and walked in, fully expecting to be snatched up by a red-cloaked guard. But he found only an empty room with a hall leading down to the depths of the structure and a stairway leading up. Josh quickly began climbing upward. He didn't stop until he had passed through a door and stood on the roof all alone.

"Why—why it's a lake!"

And so it seemed. Evidently the builders had used the ancient system of constructing a watertight roof to catch rainwater and cool the building. Except for a wall and one small rectangle in the center, the roof was like a still lake, reflecting the huge silver moon without a ripple.

"It's so pretty," Josh breathed. "But—where's the Sleeper? Must be way under the water."

Then his eyes lit on the small rectangle of stone exactly in the middle of the roof.

"That has to be it!"

Carefully Josh waded into the warm shallow water and walked across to the stone.

"Here it is!" he cried excitedly. "A door!"

It was indeed a door—a trapdoor, set in some kind of rubbery material to keep out the rain. However, Josh could not find handle or hinges.

"Well, this will be easy—or it will be impossible."

He began to say the words of the song, and, as in the past, the voice-lock clicked. Swiftly the massive steel door opened upward like the lid of a box.

In seconds Josh had descended the stairs and found the small room that contained the capsule. Without hesitation, he pushed the red button marked AWAKE. There was the hissing sound of gas escaping, and then the plastic cover swung open. Josh got his first glimpse of the fifth Sleeper—and his heart sank.

"He's not any older than I am!" he muttered in disappointment.

The Sleeper must have awakened instantly because he caught Josh's words and snapped back in a twangy accent, "Well, seems a pretty good age to me." Then he climbed out of the strange box. "Who are you, anyways?"

Josh just stared in puzzlement at the character before him. The fifth Sleeper was as tall as Josh and, as Josh had noticed, about the same age. He wore cowboy boots and a fancy Western shirt with red, green, and purple stitching that almost hurt Josh's eyes.

As if to outrage Josh still further, the newly awakened Sleeper stooped over and picked up a high-crowned straw hat with a feathered band. He clamped it down almost over his eyes with an air of satisfaction.

The hat gave him a comical effect, but the blue eyes peering out from under the broad brim were tough and steady—the type Yankee troops learned to fear at Bull Run and Missionary Ridge.

The Sleeper glanced at the capsule and shook his head. "That thing makes me as nervous as a long-tailed cat in a room full of rocking chairs!"

The comment finally stirred Josh to reply. "I'm Josh Adams. I guess you've got a lot of questions to ask—at least I did when *I* woke up."

"Well here, yes, I got some questions!" The boy's hat nodded emphatically with each word. "But guess I better introduce myself. I'm Bob Lee Jackson, but most folks just call me Reb. Course, I can see you're a Yankee, but I reckon you heard of General Bob and Stonewall."

"Who?"

Reb looked at him, then shook his head in disgust. "I'd of thought even a Yankee boy woulda heard of General Lee and General Stonewall Jackson."

"Oh, sure, I've heard of them. They were Southern leaders during the Civil War."

"Well, I'm happy you got a little learning." Reb smiled. He had a nice smile, and Josh liked the fearless look in his eyes.

"I have a lot to tell you, Reb. Look, I've got this food here, so you eat while I tell you what's going on."

"Well—some vittles might set pretty good at that. Any chitlins in that batch?"

"No, but here's some canned beef and some cans of cola."

"Shoot!" Reb complained. "Might of knowed not to trust them to pack fittin' grub."

He grumbled for a while, but Josh was amazed at the way he gobbled the food. While he ate, Josh told him what had happened—about the Uprising, the Seven Sleepers, the Sanhedrin, and then about the capture of the others.

Josh brought his tale to an end as Reb thoughtfully finished his meal. Josh could see that Reb was stunned by all the events that had taken place. At last, the Southern youth looked out from under his huge straw hat.

"You mean it's all gone, Josh? All the South really ain't there no more?"

"Not the South or the North, Reb."

He saw the pain in Reb's eyes and knew what was happening. Reb was saying good-bye to his world, just as all the Sleepers had been forced to do.

Josh wanted to shake the boy out of his grief. "But I think it'll be better someday, Reb. That's what the words say—that when the Seven Sleepers awake, the house of Goél will be filled."

"And this here Goél—who do you reckon he is?"

"I—I'm not sure. But he's not just—anybody."

"Sort of like General Lee, you mean?"

"More than General Lee, Reb. He's more than anyone."

"I'd be right proud to meet this here Goél, I reckon."

"I think you will, Reb. I think all of us will, sooner or later. But now we're in a mess. I mean, we have to find the others, then we have to get them out of jail, then—"

"Well," Reb interrupted, "I reckon finding 'em won't be no problem. Shoot! Easiest thing to find in any town is the jail."

"But how?"

"Don't they teach you Yankees nothing? Why, all you got to do is find a building with bars on the winder or a wall round it. It'll either be full of crazy people or criminals. You ought to of knowed that, Josh."

Josh grinned. It was hard not to like this flamboyant character.

"Yes, I guess I ought to have. But how do we get them out?"

"Why, shoot, Josh! It ain't really hard to get folks outta the pokey. My Grandpappy Seedy was in and outta the county jail for makin' shine so often they had a revolving door put in just for him! Shore they did! We may be livin' in some mixed-up time—but you betcha bird that if it's a jail—well, they's gotta be jailers, ain't they? And if they is jailers, they can be had, can't they?"

Josh sensed that Reb's experience with jails and police was going to be invaluable. The pair packed all the food they could carry into their pockets and left the room. Then they sneaked down the stairs and emerged in the brilliant moonlight.

"Let's just meander 'round some," Reb suggested.

Reb was enjoying the whole thing, Josh saw, in contrast to his own quaking heart.

"If anybody messes with us, they'll get whupped like a redheaded stepchild!" He pulled something from his pocket, and a sharp click followed.

Josh saw that his new friend had a six-inch switchblade in his hand. "I thought those things were illegal."

"Blamed guvmint tries to run a man's business!" Reb complained. "Tell him what to plant, and how much. And sayin' he can't make shine—and we don't stand for it. Anyways, this ain't Arkansas, is it?"

"That's right," Josh said, and he thought of his bow and of the arrow he had buried in the back of the priest. "I guess we'll have to do whatever the Quest calls for in Nuworld."

"Well, now!" Reb grinned hugely and gave Josh a staggering slap on the shoulders. "See? That's what we all said during the war when we fit you Yankees. And this time, we'll win, won't we?"

Josh seemed to see some difference between the Southern cause and evil Nuworld, but he did not think this was the time to discuss it, especially with Reb. Instead, he suggested they begin their search for the jail.

* * *

It could not have been much after midnight when they found the wall that rose up in a massive circle.

"That there is a jail, or I ain't never seen one," Reb pronounced. "Looks like the pokey down in Pine Bluff where Uncle Freeman did his last stretch. Lookit, there ain't but one big old gate, and there ain't but one little old guard. Well, ain't that a pretty come-off! They don't make jails here like they do in Arkansas."

"But, Reb, how do we get them out?"

"Well, I don't rightly know, but they's lots of ways to skin any cat. We could plant that guard, I reckon."

Josh suddenly felt a chill at Reb's offhand suggestion. "No! We can't do that! We've got to try to be better than they are—or what difference will we make in this world?"

Reb looked at Josh closely, then shrugged. "Well —you're probably right. But they is more than one way to catch a possum. Lookit this."

He pulled something out of the hip pocket of his faded jeans and waved it before Josh's eyes.

"This is Uncle Waymon's favorite skullpopper. He was the black sheep of our family. Ugly as a pan of worms! Went to being a lawman, he did. Deputy over in Garland County. But he come out of it and got himself straightened out."

The pride of Uncle Waymon was a black leather object obviously designed for hitting people over the head. Reb slapped it against his palm with a satisfactory whack.

"About ten ounces of lead in it," he confided professionally. "One tap, and they sleep like babies. Might wake up with a little headache, but that's all."

"But the guard has a helmet on," Josh protested.

"You got hands, ain't you?" Reb sniffed at Josh's ignorance and continued. "Here's what we do. We walk down and get to talkin' with the guard. You pull his hat off, and I hit him on the conk. Then sweet dreams!"

"But how do I—" Josh began to protest.

"Well, now, Josh, ain't no plan all grits and sowbelly," Reb said. "We'll think of something."

Reb walked toward the guard as if he were out for a Sunday stroll.

Josh found himself following the trail of the tall white hat.

Just before they got to the guard, Reb muttered under his breath, "You gotta get him to take his helmet off, Josh, and I'll do the necessary. It'll go finer than frog hair!"

Suddenly they were in front of the gate, and Josh was looking into a pair of eyes the color of spit, mean and dangerous. The guard placed the top of a wicked-looking pike at Josh's chest and said something in Nuworld, but Josh could not catch it. Josh noticed that the guard was looking at him and that Reb had stepped to one side, his hand in his back pocket. He could hear the whistle of an owl, and the moon turned the world to silver—especially the guard's helmet that gleamed a tough, steely gray.

Josh's mind was an absolute blank. The only thing he was conscious of was the tip of the pike pushing against his chest. Then, without any forethought at all, Josh slipped to his knees and stretched out full length as if in a faint.

The guard uttered an exclamation of surprise. He bent over to examine Josh more closely.

Through the slits of his half-closed eyes, Josh saw the guard above him, blotting out the silver moon. Without hesitation, he reached out and yanked off the guard's helmet.

Twenty things could have gone wrong—the helmet strap could have been fastened, Josh could have missed his grasp—but there were no hitches, and the helmet slipped off easily. At once there was the solid thud of Reb's blackjack on the guard's head.

Immediately the guard fell across Josh, pinning him to the ground. Then the weight of the unconscious man shifted as Reb dragged him off.

"Well, now—" Reb chuckled "—ain't that a caution, Josh? Worked slicker than boiled okra, didn't it? Help me get this innocent back here in the shadows."

They dragged the limp form under a shrub.

"Now don't you fret about *him*—Uncle Waymon spent lots of time learnin' me about the skullpopper. I give him a four-hour tap, so we got plenty a time."

Josh looked at Reb's merry eyes beneath the tall hat. "Reb, if all the Confederate soldiers were like you, I don't see how you lost the war."

It was the highest compliment Josh could pay. He saw that Reb sensed this and smiled.

"You'd better get on with that rat-killing." Reb grinned and punched Josh on the arm in affection. "What's next?"

Josh thought hard, then said, "I'll go open that gate and go inside. I'll find the prisoners if I can. Now somebody else—another guard—may come. If they do, you give some kind of call—like an owl, maybe? And I'll know that the way out is blocked."

It wasn't a very good plan. Reb's eyes widened in astonishment. "And you'll be trapped in there, and them madder'n roped coons!"

"It's the best I can think of, Reb," Josh explained apologetically.

Reb thought for a moment, then grinned again.

"I'm proud to know you, Yankee. Always wondered how you whupped us, but if them Yankees was like you, reckon I can see. Get along with you."

Josh walked toward the gate. The warmth of Reb's approval cheered him a little. Yet he still felt cold inside. What lay on the other side of the gate? Would he be able to open it, or was there a key? And how would he ever find his friends?

But there was no lock on the gate—just a simple steel sliding bar. He reached out and slid it back. Now the way was clear. But was something on the other side? Guards? Fierce watchdogs? What?

Once again he murmured Goél's name, and the door swung open.

Or perhaps he did not say it, for as soon as the door opened, a form was there falling against him, and he felt two arms around his neck. In Josh's ear, Sarah was saying over and over, "Goél! Goél!"

13

The Trap

None of the Sanhedrin, even the eldest, could remember seeing Chief Interrogator Elmas in such a rage. Those who could, fled. Others were compelled to remain in the council room and be flayed by his words, words that Elmas used like whips.

"Perhaps you have tired of the easy life," he screamed at the cowering priests. "That can be changed! If you do not find these—Sleepers" —he spat the word out as if it were an obscenity— "you will find out what it is like to receive the attentions of our Questioner!"

Although they all flinched at the suggestion, one of them, named Bolus—a little bolder than the others—asked, "But, Master, why are these Oldworlders so important? They're only children."

Bolus would have done better to have poured gasoline on a fire. Elmas rose up, then swelled like a monstrous toad. His face glowed with rage as he screamed, "Only children, are they? You *dunce*! Don't you know that once in Oldworld a baby was born in a lowly place—just a common child like these—and that one child wrenched the entire world from our grasp!"

Elmas turned away in sour disgust and then sat down. When he spoke again, his voice was icy cold. "You are on trial here, brothers," he warned. "What do you propose to keep your fat carcasses out of the mines?"

There was silence.

Then a smooth voice stirred the room. "Master, I believe I can do something."

A figure dressed in green stepped out from behind a pillar shadowed in darkness. Hamar slowly approached the council.

It was obvious that here was no escaped prisoner. Hamar lounged carelessly in front of the Chief Interrogator, unlike the cowering priests.

"You!" Elmas started up, his face burning with anger. "You are to blame for all this. I have several surprises for you, snakemaster!"

"Oh, no, Master, I think not," Hamar answered coolly.

The others gasped, and Elmas opened his mouth to have Hamar stripped to the bone.

But Hamar spoke before the Chief Interrogator could utter a word. "After all, Master, it was I who brought them to you."

"And they are lost!" Elmas snarled.

"No, not really." Hamar smiled. "Gone, yes, but that's the fault of your guards. And if you had killed them—as you wanted to do—there would still be Sleepers to contend with in the future. There are seven of them, you know."

"But how will we get them back?" Elmas demanded.

"It shouldn't be difficult. One of them is an egotistical fool—the one called Dave. I fed his ego and introduced him to hypnosis, although he was not aware of it. Now his mind is in my grasp. I can contact him at any time, and he will answer."

Elmas slowly relaxed and spoke through an evil chuckle. "He wanted to play with magic, did he?"

"Most fools do, Master—spells, astrology, hypnotism—they love the mysteries."

"Until they are sucked under and fall into our power, eh?" Elmas said, flashing a wicked smile. "When can we reach them?"

"I will touch his mind tonight," Hamar said. "He'll think he's seeing me, and I'll lead him right back to the Temple. Then the Questioner shouldn't have too much trouble finding out the rest, eh?"

"No trouble at all," Elmas said suavely. "Let me know when you have them. There'll be something in this for you, friend Hamar."

"My only motive is to serve the Sanhedrin and you." Hamar smiled.

"Of course," Elmas agreed smoothly.

* * *

But while Elmas and Hamar were plotting, the ragged band of fugitives were having a meeting of their own. They had hidden just outside the city in a grove of large oak trees. After their ordeal in the prison, they had needed time to rest and recover.

However, feasting on nuts, berries, and a scrawny pig that Reb had somehow managed to capture had done little for their bodies. And Josh saw that their spirits were famished too. He read defeat in most of the travelers' faces.

Although his own spirit was heavy, he tried to cheer his companions. "Well, where's the next Sleeper? About time to think of that. Only two more to go and then—"

"Then what?" Dave snapped.

"Why, when the Seventh Sleeper awakes, why . . ." Josh's voice trailed off. He did not know the answer.

"We'll have two more mouths to feed," Mat barked.

Sarah slipped close to Josh. Ever since they had met at the prison gate, he had seen a special trust in her eyes for him.

"Something will happen—I just know it will, Josh!"

"Something will happen all right," Dave said quickly with a jealous look at Josh. "We'll get caught and locked up. And this time, there won't be any escape."

135

"I think you're right," Mat said. "Look here." He pointed at the map spread out on the ground. "Look where the next Sleeper is." He tapped the map. "Right in the midst of the Deadlands. See? The song has a key of 16 and 8. That will be right here in the middle of the desert."

"Is right," Kybus grunted. "My people live not too far. Bad place for people. Dry, hot, and dead."

Josh looked round and saw discouragement on every face. Even Tam and Volka were drained. He tried to muster the words that would encourage hope.

"We won't fail. Goél will make a way for us."

Just the name of Goél seemed to encourage most of them for a moment. The two Gemini brightened. The rush of encouragement then spread to the others.

But Dave said loudly, "Look, Josh, I'm not putting you down, but this is life and death. None of us has ever seen this Goél. And you admit that you were in pretty bad shape when you saw him. You probably were just hallucinating or dreaming. That's natural when you're bone-tired and desperate. But we can't run this operation on fantasies. So I say we pull back and wait. Let the excitement die down. Then—why, we might even negotiate."

"No!" came Crusoe's weak voice. The old man pulled himself up and stared at Dave with his sunken eyes. "No one can negotiate with them—you cannot bargain with evil. It will devour you!" His words poured out in a fury. Then, drained and empty, Crusoe fell back.

Josh wanted to speak, but Dave beat him to it.

"Look, let's not get angry. We all want the same thing. But look at this map. See, here is the Sixth Sleeper. I agree that we can probably muddle through the Deadlands, but how do we get from there to the Seventh Sleeper? It must be several hundred miles—and over deserts—"

"And through or over the Hogbacks," Kybus said. "Can't climb those. I see many peoples die there."

"Just what I say!" Dave cried.

"But we can't just quit," Josh protested.

"Shoot, no!" Reb shouted. "Old Stonewall one time, why he marched a bunch of Rebs clear round the whole Union army! Why, we can raise more racket than a pig if'n we get to it!"

Dave obviously didn't like Reb, had disliked him from the first, so his response was predictable. "That will hardly do here," he snapped at the Southerner. "Those were soldiers. We're just a bunch of teenagers and fr—"

"Wait a minute," Josh said. A glimmer of light had come to him. "I remember something—something my dad told me just before I went to sleep."

"What was it, Josh?" Crusoe rose up on one elbow, his eyes gleaming.

"He said, 'Obey the book.'" Josh was silent. "It was about the last thing he ever told me. I—I wish he were here."

"What book?" Sarah asked.

"And I've just remembered something else. The last thing Mom wrote in her journal."

"What is it, Josh?" Crusoe asked.

Josh fished out the well-worn journal, opened it to the last entry, and began reading.

Josh, I've been praying for you this night. Somehow I know that someday you'll be in a terribly dangerous situation. All hope will be gone, and you'll be almost ready to quit. Here is what I want to say to you: Don't take counsel of your fears! You will not be lost! Somehow I know that as I write these words. My counsel is: Think of the eagles, how they mount up on strong wings. Remember the bald eagle we saw when we

137

were on vacation in Wyoming? How he beat his great pinions and rose up high over the mountains? Somehow you will rise over your crisis like that great eagle. Think of the eagle, Josh!

A heavy silence fell after Josh finished.

Finally Dave said, "Well, I can't see that that helps us."

"What is 'eagles'?" Kybus asked.

"Big birds," Josh said. "Great big birds."

Kybus did not say anything, but he was thinking, Josh saw. He also saw that he would never get them all to agree, so he said firmly, "Let's go. We can make a few hours before dark."

"I think we ought to vote," Dave argued.

"No vote, Dave," Josh said, looking him right in the eye and wishing that he felt as firm inside as his voice sounded. "This is the time when somebody has to decide. If I have to fight you again, I will."

"Shoot, Josh, let me do it," Reb eagerly volunteered. "I'll whop this—"

"OK, OK." Dave threw up his hands. "Just remember, I was against it from the start."

The rest of the day was misery for Josh. He began to question his own actions, but he found no answers. Despondently, he surveyed the little band. There were the Sleepers—himself, Dave, Sarah, Jake, and Reb. Then there were the Nuworlders—Crusoe, Volka, Mat and Tam, Rama and Amar, the three Hunters, and Kybus. Fifteen in all. A tiny group of fifteen against all the might of the Sanhedrin. Josh wearily shook his head and vowed to think only of the road ahead.

Just before dark, the travelers paused in the depths of an old forest and gathered around a small fire. There they began eating what was nearly the last of their food.

No one spoke much. Reb sat close to Sarah, telling her tall tales about his Uncle Seedy. Dave stared moodily into the dark gloom of the forest. Just before Josh dozed off, Kybus asked, "How big is eagles?"

But he didn't remember answering before he dropped off to sleep. He only remembered wondering if the next Sleeper would be any more help than the others.

* * *

Dave slept less soundly. He tried to shut out the voice. Yet, no matter how he turned or held his hands over his ears, the voice persisted.

"Dave! Wake up, Dave!"

Dave finally opened his eyes to prove to himself that he was only dreaming. But there in the darkness, broken only by the flickering light of the dying fire, stood Hamar.

"Hamar!" Dave cried and sat up quickly. "How did you get here? How did you get out of the prison?"

"I'll tell you all about that later." Hamar's voice sounded a little fuzzy, but Dave's ears were ringing with the lack of sleep.

"I've been trying to catch up with you for a long time. Come on, we've got to hurry."

"What do you mean? Where are we going?"

"We have to help your friends, Dave. Look at them! They're all in a trance. You couldn't wake them if you tried."

Dave's head was swimming, but he could see that the others were absolutely motionless. "But what are we—"

Hamar's voice was soothing, and Dave felt himself drawn to this wise man who had some answers.

"Dave, you've got to help them. If you don't, they're done for—all of you, for that matter. If you'll come with me, I'll show you how to save them. We don't have time to argue."

139

Dave was caught in a difficult position. He was afraid, but his pride was hurt so badly that he would do anything to show the others that *he* was right. Yet a nagging feeling remained that he was doing the wrong thing.

I know they don't trust Hamar, said Dave to himself. *But this is for their own good.*

"Come along, Dave," Hamar whispered.

Dave got to his feet, drawn by the man's strange power. He felt that his mind was locked into Hamar's command. He followed the piper into the darkness of the woods without so much as a backward glance at his friends.

For hours Dave followed Hamar through the forest toward the city. Sometimes the piper would disappear, then return and draw him on. Always Hamar's voice encouraged him.

"Come along, Dave. That's right, keep coming. You're almost there."

For Dave, it was like being drawn into a dark whirlpool. At first he had been on the edge at the widest part of the circle. But gradually he moved inward, closer and closer to the dark center of the maelstrom. Something told him to resist, but he was caught in the flow, and on and on and down and down he went.

Finally, when Dave could walk no more, and his body cried out in protest, he saw a light.

Hamar's voice was very strong now. "We're there, Dave."

The light grew brighter.

Then Dave came to the light, and he saw that it was Hamar himself, holding a torch high. There was an evil smile on the piper's face as he spoke. "You've come to me, haven't you, boy? Now, we can find the other Sleepers."

And then Dave knew it all, for he saw the red-robed priests standing behind Hamar. He saw the Questioner with a bright, shining steel instrument in his hand. Dave realized that he had betrayed everything he loved.

He awoke as cruel hands grasped him with a touch that went to the bone. He cried out. But there was no ear to hear or heart to care as he voiced his agony to the darkness.

14

The Sixth Sleeper

D ave is gone!"
Josh tried to go back to sleep, but the voice persisted.

"Dave is gone, Josh." He forced his eyes open and saw Sarah standing over him. Quickly he sat up and looked to the spot where Dave had been. Nothing!

"He's gone, Josh," Sarah repeated. "And Kybus is gone too."

Josh shook the sleep from his head, trying to think.

"But there's nowhere for them to go!"

"I think Dave's gone back to the Temple," Crusoe said.

Josh saw that the whole group was up and awake.

"I think he's going to betray us to the Sanhedrin, Josh."

"He wouldn't do that!" Sarah protested.

"What makes you think that, Crusoe?" Josh asked.

"He's been *different,*" Crusoe said. "I can't explain it, but I've seen that kind of change occur many times. The enemy is clever, and when they find a willing mind, they can—bend it. Dave was off guard, and he doesn't know the power of the Sanhedrin. They can trap the mind, and then the body *has* to follow."

Crusoe seemed to shrink a little, and his own frail body appeared even more vulnerable. "I've fought the enemy for years, and I know this—they will take the soul that lets them into the mind. Josh, we must leave!"

"Where's Kybus?" Jake asked.

The others looked around, but the dwarf was indeed gone.

"Well, looks like the population is declining," Jake commented.

"We can't be too far from the next Sleeper," Josh said.

"What are you hoping for?" Jake asked. "Do you really think that this Sleeper—or the last one—will have all the answers?"

"I—I don't know, Jake. But we can't go back. What else is left?"

There was a slight murmur of agreement, and Josh quickly tried to skip over their losses and doubts. "Now—where are we? How close to the Sleeper?"

"Not too far," Tam said.

"Yes—very far," Mat argued glumly. "Ten miles distance all right, but after only a mile walk we leave the woods and begin crossing the desert. Stones are like razors there, and it gets hot enough to fry an egg on the rocks."

"Here's the song," Sarah said.

> *"I am a lock without a key—*
> *I guard my treasure silently.*
>
> *"No man that breathes*
> *may pass through me.'"*

"That's 16 across and 8 down—see? Right here." Josh pointed.

"Well, if we're going, let's go," Mat concluded.

The travelers gathered their small supply of food and blankets and trudged through the trees without more talk. Nearly two hours passed before they made their way out of the woods and into scrubby forest. Then the ground quickly turned to sandy loam, spotted with low plants.

144

Finally, they reached the edge of the real desert. The sun had risen only two hours before, but already the heat poured over the plain.

"Pull your coats or handkerchiefs over your faces," Crusoe said. "We should wait until night, but we don't have time. Are all the water bags and canteens filled?"

"Shore," Reb said. "I reckon that sun ain't no hotter'n an Arkansas sun. As Uncle Seedy used to say, it can't be no worse than sliding down a forty-foot razor blade into a vat of alcohol!"

The passage through the Ghost Marshes had been terrible, but this was just as bad. Josh could feel the moisture being cooked out of his body, and the water they carried had to be conserved. The Hunters were sent out to watch for enemies or water, and they skimmed the land like hunting dogs.

"I'd shore like to have them fellers 'long on a real hunt," Reb said admiringly.

It was late in the afternoon, and the sun was sinking, when they found the sixth Sleeper. They had stopped to rest under the shade of a large rock formation, one of the few they had seen, when Sarah said suddenly, "This is it!"

"This is what?" Josh asked.

"This is where the Sleeper is—or close by. Look at the heart."

They leaned closer and saw that the tiny heart was fully aglow.

Josh looked around. "But where? I don't see a thing."

"Then it must be in this rock," Jake said. "Let's look for a door—a hidden door."

"It's just like a story, ain't it, Sarah?" Reb said. Then he uttered a shrill cry. *"Ow!"*

"What's wrong, Reb?" Sarah asked.

"Just 'bout knocked my toe off on this here root—no, 'tain't a root neither."

145

He bent over, then gave what must have been his idea of a rebel cry. "It's a handle—to a door!"

The travelers all spilled around him and began to scoop back the sand. Soon a square, steel door with a plain handle lay in the clear.

"Well, *that* was easy," Josh said in relief. "Let's get inside. Let me see the words to that song, Sarah."

He read them out carefully, and the door swung open at once with a soft sigh.

"Well, strip me naked an' hide my clothes! Ain't that a caution!" Reb exclaimed admiringly.

Before they could stop him, Reb stooped and started to enter the dark door. Then with a cry he fell backward, as if struck by lightning.

"Reb! What is it?" Josh cried, as they gathered around him.

The Southerner was trembling, and his hat had fallen to the ground, revealing his pale, sun-bleached hair.

"I'm OK, but don't nobody go through that door. It's electric. Like to of knocked my head off."

Cautiously, Josh reached his hand into the opening and drew it back with a yelp.

"It's wired," he confirmed.

The company stood helplessly in front of the open door.

"Well, what now?" Mat asked. "We can't stay here long."

Josh opened his mouth, but nothing came out. He could not think of one single answer. Finally he said heavily, "I—I just don't know."

Sarah must have seen how close to tears he was. She quickly said, "Let's eat a bite and have some water. We'll think of something. Volka, put Mr. Crusoe in the shade while we get the food."

146

Sarah kept everyone busy with little chores to fend off discouragement. The Hunters came in, and while they were eating they spoke in Nuworld to Crusoe. It was obvious that what they said disturbed the old man.

He turned to them and said, "The Hunters have spotted a party coming across the desert. I fear it's the Sanhedrin."

Josh said, "What will we do, Mr. Crusoe?"

"I don't know, my boy. We will have to trust."

"I have it!" Sarah cried and jumped to her feet.

"What is it, Sarah? What's wrong?" her friends began to ask.

"Oh, why don't we just listen to the song?" she cried in a mixture of joy and anger. "The answer is so simple. *'No man that breathes may pass through me.'* What does that mean?" she demanded.

"I reckon only dead men can get in there," Reb answered.

"No! Listen to the words. No *man* may pass through. *Man.* But I'm not a man—so I can pass through."

Sarah ran to the door. Before anyone could do more than cry out a warning, she had disappeared into the opening.

The others looked at each other in shocked surprise.

"That is some fine lady," Jake said in admiration.

"I reckon I'd take her to the ice cream social anytime," Reb said.

Josh made no comment. Instead, he kept his eyes glued to the door. Sarah's bravery was admirable, but who knew what was in there? It could be a trap of some kind.

"I don't like it," he muttered finally.

"It'll be OK, Josh," Tam said. "Sarah will be fine."

"If something doesn't eat her, or if she doesn't get caught in some kind of trap, or—"

Mat was off on a list of catastrophes, when Josh snapped at him. "I wish you'd keep quiet, Mat!"

They waited anxiously.

Finally Jake spoke. "I see something coming out."

They all edged close, and two figures emerged, Sarah in front, and just behind her the sixth Sleeper—once again, not a muscular soldier or a formidable fighter. No, the sixth Sleeper stepped into the sun, blinking her eyes against the sudden light. She was the prettiest girl that Josh had ever seen.

"Hello," she said huskily. "My name is Abigail." And when she smiled, every masculine heart within twenty yards beat a little faster.

15

On the Wings of Eagles

Sarah looked on with disgust as the dark-haired Abbey sat on a rock with a clump of teenage males at her feet. They looked up at her with bright eyes as they told her all that had happened. Jake, Reb, and Josh sat in the front row with the Oldworld creatures not far behind. As Abbey smiled at them, there was an audible gasp from the audience.

"Well, Sarah," Crusoe said, watching her keenly. "Don't you want to help our newest recruit get acquainted with Nuworld?"

Sarah knew Crusoe read her jealousy, but she couldn't hide her disgust. "Look at them staring at her." She stamped her foot impatiently. "Here we are about to be caught, sentenced to certain death, and all those fools can do is drool over a pretty face."

"Well, she is a fine-looking girl, Sarah." Crusoe smiled. "She can't help that, can she?"

"No, but she could—she could—oh, I don't know!"

Suddenly Sarah began to feel tears stream down her face. She threw herself into Crusoe's thin arms.

Sarah had endured heat, hunger, danger, and other terrible things. Why would she cry over this girl she hardly knew?

Crusoe did not seem particularly worried. He smiled and murmured, "Don't worry, Sarah. Abbey is a beautiful girl, but you have the ornament of a humble, yet proud, spirit. That's what Josh—and the others—see in you."

Sarah wanted to say, "I'd rather have her long eye-lashes." But instead she said, "Mr. Crusoe, what will happen to us? I mean, there's no way that we can get away if the Hunters are right."

"Not in the practical sense, child," Crusoe said. "But you know, I found out one thing about this world, and no one wants to hear it."

"I do," said Sarah, leaning against him.

"Well, you will hear it then. Boiled down to one sentence, here it is: We learn little from good times, Sarah. We learn through difficult times."

Sarah suddenly laughed. "Well, we ought to be learning *now!*"

She left Crusoe, and soon the group around Abbey broke up and re-formed around the small campfire.

"Ain't it dangerous to have a campfire?" Reb asked.

"I don't think so," Crusoe answered. "If the attack force of the Sanhedrin is coming this way, they will find us."

"What will we do then?" Josh asked.

"I don't know, Josh. But this may be our last time together, so I want to say one thing to all of you—especially to you Sleepers. Something is being shaken in Nuworld. And you are at the heart of it."

They all leaned forward to listen to the old man. Only the lonely sound of a desert fox broke the silence.

"Tomorrow may bring grief, but you must learn to kiss joy as it flies. Do not try to hang onto pleasures. They are all of the moment." He looked at them with a prophetic fire in his fine old eyes. "The world is bent and ruined. It has been waiting for something—all of creation is standing on tiptoe, waiting! You are the hope of the world."

"But we're likely to be dead or in jail tomorrow," Jake protested.

"Goél has caused you Sleepers to be protected and to be raised up at this time and in this place. It is your hour. *It is the hour of the House of Goél.*"

"What is that?" Sarah asked.

"The House of Goél is man—man as he *should* be. In these days, all peoples on earth will come to fill his house. And you stand as a sign, my children, that the House is ready, the doors are open. The invitation is in your hands."

This speech seemed to have drained the old man of his frail strength, for he slumped back onto his blanket. The others looked at him, then at one another.

Finally Reb hesitantly remarked, "My land, looks like we're somebody, don't it?"

None of them slept much that night, and, just before dawn, Sarah felt Josh come to sit beside her as she stared into the east, waiting for sunrise.

She could not resist saying, "Well, did you finally get Her Majesty brought up to date?" Instantly, she regretted her cheap and mean remark.

Josh didn't answer for a moment. Then he sighed and asked, "Are you mad at me, Sarah?"

"No," she said and hurriedly averted her embarrassed face. "I'm just silly and tired and selfish. Don't pay any attention to my moods."

"Sarah," Josh said slowly, "I might as well tell you. I'm scared to death."

He hung his head and grasped a handful of sand in his fist. "I know I ought to be brave and all that—but I can't help feeling scared," Josh continued. Slowly he let the sand trickle through his fingers.

"Well, join the club." Sarah gently slipped her arm around his shoulders. "Don't you know we're all scared?"

"Not Reb or Jake," Josh objected. "And Dave wouldn't be, either."

151

"Oh, no? You're just being honest." She paused, then said, "Josh, just in case something happens tomorrow —and I know everything will be fine—but anyway, I want to tell you something. I want you to know how much I like you. I always have liked you, Josh, even in the other world."

"You do!" Josh sat up and looked at her. "But I'm so plain and ordinary. I'm always saying the wrong thing—"

"And you're always putting yourself down," Sarah finished. "I just wanted to tell you—just in case—"

Josh seemed to want to say something to Sarah, but after her confession she hurriedly slipped away, and the opportunity passed.

* * *

Soon the sun was up, and one of the Hunters—the one with the bulging eyes—said something that Josh couldn't understand. He looked where the Hunter was pointing and saw a thin stream of dust. Josh jumped to his feet.

"Here, everyone. Get your bows ready. You have your swords? Now, Volka, you watch that side, and the Hunters . . ."

He continued to post them around the pile of rocks that formed a natural circle, but Mat said, "Josh, we won't last five minutes."

"Well, that five minutes will be ours and not theirs." Josh's rebellious spirit began to infect them all, and soon the company had developed a defense strategy.

By the time their plans were complete, the procession marching across the desert had come so close that Josh and his group could see the glint of their steel-tipped spears. The procession stopped, and the enemy began to fan out in a circle.

"They're going to surround us," Josh warned. "Be ready."

His hope lay in the archers, but there were only four who were adept with bows, and arrows were scarce. Volka could destroy anything in his reach, but he would never be able to get close enough under the enemy's bow-fire.

Finally the circle was complete. The enemy started to close in. Arrows began to whiz over the travelers' heads, but Josh told the group to hold its fire. "Wait until they're closer!"

The enemy was well-trained, however. They were not wasting men or ammunition. They drew back after one of them was wounded by an arrow from Mat's bow.

"Reckon they're going to wait us out," Reb said. "Sure wish I had my old .30-30 for 'bout five minutes. I'd settle their hash."

All morning they waited and grew more and more thirsty. Finally the long-sighted Hunter spotted more dust to the east and spoke to Crusoe.

"I would say they're bringing up heavy equipment —shields and rolling turrets, I'd guess." Crusoe spoke without a trace of despondency, and yet Josh's heart ached when he heard the fatigue in the old man's voice.

Crusoe's astuteness hadn't dimmed, however. He seemed to guess Josh's thoughts and softly remarked, "No, Josh, there must always be some hope."

Josh knew the rest had all been pretending to believe that hope remained. They had been calling out encouragement to each other all the long, undying morning. But now, with this new threat, it all seemed futile. The arrows fired by the enemy snapped at the rocks.

Josh's thirst grew almost unbearable. And the dust cloud grew larger. "They'll be here in an hour," he croaked.

Then something happened. One of the enemy stepped out and called, "Adams! Joshua Adams!"

"What is it? Who wants me?"

"You are trapped, Adams," the soldier said. "In thirty minutes we will have protection, and you will all be either dead or captured. I will make you a proposition. If you will surrender now, I will help you. The Chief Interrogator will listen to me. Why should you die uselessly? Surrender!"

"Don't listen to him, Josh," Sarah pleaded.

"I won't—but he's right. We only have a few minutes. I—I wish I could do something. We've gone through all this, and I don't want to die for nothing—"

Suddenly there was a cry. "Look! Look up in the sky."

Josh looked up and thought he was losing his mind, for coming from nowhere was a large flight of eagles!

"The eagles come," Volka said in his deep voice. "Just like the promise."

Now they were closer, and Josh could see that a number of the huge birds had something around their necks. Then he saw that small people were riding on the backs of the eagles.

"What kind of bird is that?" Jake asked in stunned amazement.

"I guess they're the kind that's going to get us out of here," Reb said. Then he gave a rebel yell and threw his straw hat as high as he could. "I shore wish Uncle Seedy was here to see this!"

"Look at the enemy!" Mat said. "They're running!" And so they were. As the eagles circled above, their tiny riders fired a deadly rain of arrows on the Sanhedrin's Servants. Bodies began to drop. The survivors fled the scene like so many rabbits.

With open mouth, Josh watched one large bird land ten feet in front of him.

A voice said, "I bring eagles, just like old book say, eh?" A crumpled figure slipped from a saddle on the mighty bird's back and ran forward to grab Josh.

"Kybus!" Josh cried out and hugged the little gnome in a wild dance. "But where did you come from? And what are these birds?"

"My people sometimes called Birdpeople. We tame birds, and they serve us. We their friends. These our riding birds."

They were not true eagles, Josh saw, but some kind of condor. Even in the Oldworld, eagles had been very large, but these birds had wings that must have spanned twenty-five feet. They had beaks large enough to bite a man in two, but they did not seem fierce at all.

"When I hear 'bout eagles, I know I can go to my people, and they come for us. Come, we go now."

"Go where?" Josh asked.

"To seventh Sleeper. There!"

Kybus pointed across the deserts to snowcapped peaks.

"Beyond mountains is place you show on map. No can walk—we fly. Come, everyone get one, and we fly."

The other travelers had come close enough to hear. Soon it became clear that they were going to have to mount the huge birds and ride them high in the sky.

"I get airsick," Abbey complained.

"Then you better take a plastic bag," Josh said coolly. "We're all going, and that's the end of it."

"Whoooee!" Reb shouted. "I been to three county fairs and four snake-stompings, but I ain't never seen nothing like *this*!"

In no time, they were all mounted. It was rather frightening, Josh found, to meet the beady eyes of the bird he mounted and to be so close to that steely beak. But at the same time, it was fun to feel the soft, feathery body filled with muscles, muscles as taut and strong as steel wires, ready to lift its rider to freedom.

"Wait a minute," he said. "What about Volka? He's too big for an eagle to carry—and we can't leave him here."

"No worry," Kybus said. "He go with us. You watch."

Then Josh saw that four of the large eagles had been yoked together with a sort of harness, all the lines running to Volka, who was wearing something that looked like an old-fashioned corset.

"He heavy cargo," Kybus said, "but they carry him. Now, we go! Is time!"

Then, just as the heavy equipment of the enemy came into range, there was a ruffle of mighty wings, and Josh felt the body of his great condor tense. In a second, he was airborne!

The earth faded away, and the wings beat down, then rose again. The air cooled his face. Josh and his friends soared higher and higher. He smiled as the tiny men below shook their fists. Their curses faded as the eagles soared upward.

Josh glanced across at the closest bird and saw Sarah, her face pale but a look of wild joy in her eyes.

"I guess the book was right," she called out. "I like this mounting up with wings of eagles."

Josh nodded and turned to see Volka being towed along easily by the four great birds. All the others were clinging to the backs of their eagles, and Reb was sitting straight up, waving his straw hat over his head.

"Hi-yo, Silver, away!" he shouted at the top of his lungs.

Oldworld, Josh thought, had never been like this!

16
The Seventh Sleeper

What a trip that was! Imagine sitting astride a horse, but with no hard hoofs jolting you at each step. Instead, there is only the smooth beat of mighty wings that drive you through the thin air. The flight is so smooth that you hear only the wind blowing across your face!

At first there is fear—for the earth has fallen away into distant geometric patterns, and one slip will end it all. But finally the mind relaxes, and you can sit straight and look down at the earth with the freedom of the bird himself.

The tiny hairline far to the south is the tumbling Roaring Horse River. That far distant gleam is the gold turret of the Temple where the Chief Interrogator, Elmas, sits plotting your doom. But all his dark power cannot rise to the clouds that you now plunge into.

The dream of flight has become a solid reality. You emerge from the clouds to see a rocky needle rising sheer out of the desert, pointing a stony finger to the heavens.

"There it is," Josh yelled, pointing at the needle. "That's got to be it."

Kybus pulled his eagle over to the right of Josh as easily as any cowboy ever maneuvered a horse. "Yah— that is Needle. We be there in maybe twenty minutes," he promised.

Josh was sorry the flight was over when they began to descend. But the sight of the stone buildings, or ruins, where the final Sleeper lay reminded him that this was the end of the Quest.

The giant condors came to earth gently, and all the riders scrambled off onto the ground.

"Now, birds go back," Kybus said, and Josh watched nervously as the birds took flight. Slowly the huge condors disappeared back in the direction of Kybus's land.

"Wow!" Reb sighed. "That was some ride, boy!" He looked over the side of the Needle and whistled low. "Watch out for that first step—it's a humdinger!"

So it was, for the flat top of the mountain stopped abruptly and fell away to the desert floor far below. Several footpaths had been hacked out of the plateau's side, but nothing else.

"We'll be safe here—for a while," Crusoe said. "But the Chief Interrogator will be coming sooner or later. And they can starve us out if they have to."

"But how will they know where we are?" Sarah asked.

"Dave will have told them. He knows all the locations of the Sleepers."

"I—can't understand Dave. I thought he was one of us," Sarah said in a soft, grieved voice.

Crusoe nodded slowly. "He was, Sarah, but there is only one defense against the sin of pride—the shield of humility."

"Hadn't we better find the Sleeper?" Josh asked anxiously. "You know, I've thought every time we found a capsule that our leader would be waiting inside. But I really think this one must be it. It makes sense," he argued. "This is the last Sleeper, and here we are, stuck on the point of a needle with no way out. Now Goél couldn't expect the first six of us to do anything like saving the world. We're not even adults yet. So I think the seventh Sleeper will be the one who will pull everything together."

"Hey, you could be right," Jake said. "Let's find that capsule." He pointed at the ruins of an ancient building. "I bet it's there somewhere. Check your heart, Sarah."

"It's on fire right now!" Sarah said, and she began to run toward the building. "Yes! This is the way." The stones of the building were old beyond knowledge, rounded and stained with time. The roof had fallen in, and some of the large round pillars that supported it were leaning outward dangerously. But Josh and the others rushed inside without hesitation.

The room inside was very large, possibly one hundred feet square, and arches from the pillars supported the high ceiling. Slits along the apex allowed light inside. The whole place looked like an open air theater. High on one wall was a sentence formed out of carved stones:

YOU SHALL KNOW THE TRUTH
AND THE TRUTH
SHALL MAKE YOU FREE

The travelers had not been there for more than a few seconds when one of the Hunters discovered a steel door set in the wall. They all fell over each other to reach it.

Then Josh said, "Sarah, read the words of the song."

Sarah got out her paper and read the verse slowly:

"'I sleep—

"'in that thin air
where eagles dare!'"

The door slowly swung up, and Josh held his breath as they all pressed toward the chamber that held the capsule. There was room only for Crusoe and the Sleepers, but the rest peered in through the entrance as Josh held his finger on the AWAKE button.

"Here we go," he breathed.

He touched the button. There was the sound of escaping gas, then the cover swung back, and the seventh Sleeper, he who was to lead them all out of tribulation, sat up and stared at them. There was a moment of total silence. Then the last Sleeper spoke.

"So what's happening, people?"

He was possibly the youngest of the Sleepers, certainly the smallest. He wore a pair of rugged jeans, tennis shoes, and a khaki T-shirt. His rich, full hair was bound back by a yellow headband. And his skin was as black as night itself.

"You don't say?" he finally prodded them. "That bad, hm?"

Josh glanced at Reb's face. He saw that his friend's usual smile had disappeared. His eyes had become narrow slits.

"Just what we need—"

"Wait a minute, Reb," Josh interrupted quickly. "I guess he's as shocked as we are. What's your name? I'm Josh."

The new Sleeper bowed from his sitting position. "Mine is Gregory Randolf Washington Jones." His teeth flashed. Then he gracefully climbed out of the box and slid to the floor. "But most just calls me 'Wash.'"

"Well," Josh said a little lamely, "you're not exactly what we were expecting, Wash."

"So I see." Wash grinned. "Likewise, I was expecting the new world when I came around." He stopped when he spied Reb's suspicious face. "But this looks pretty much the same as the old one to me."

Sarah moved a little closer to him and smiled warmly. "Don't worry, Wash," she said and put her hand out. "I'm Sarah. And I believe you were right, thinking you'd see some kind of new world. All of us human types are minority material in this place. Let me introduce you to the real Nuworld folks out here."

She led them all out of the tiny chamber and said, "First, your fellow Sleepers. This is Abbey, Jake, and Reb —you've already met Josh. That's Volka, and Tam and Mat, and Amar and Rama, and these three are the Hunters, and this is Kybus."

Wash's small face was a study as he looked at the giant, the dwarfs, and all the rest of the strange crew. Finally he screwed his face up into a squint and said, "I can see I've got some catching up to do."

"And we've got some rethinking to do," Reb said sullenly. "Is this your great leader, Josh? Cause I ain't havin' none of it. We need *him* like a pig needs a saddle!"

"I don't understand it either, Reb, but Wash isn't here by accident—none of us are."

"The House of Goél won't be filled with one color, Reb," a voice said. They turned to see that Crusoe was sitting with his back against the stone wall, his face pale as paper. "It will be a large House, and it will have people in it far different from us. Goél is not for one people, but for *all* people!"

But Crusoe's words fell on dull ears. Paradoxically, it was just at this point that Josh—and the other Sleepers and travelers—should have been most confident. Their mission was complete, wasn't it? The prophecy had said that when the Sleepers awoke, the House of Goél would be filled. But nothing seemed to have changed. In the face of their apparent failure, the group was plunged into the deepest gloom.

Perhaps they had all expected too much from the last Sleeper, for all looked a little angry or disappointed at the innocent Wash. They had been tuned to open the last door and have victory walk into their arms. But instead, there seemed to be no answers and only more problems.

The disbelief in their faces seemed to infect the very air of the ancient temple. Josh tried to fight against it, but the hopelessness of the situation swamped his heart with despair. "I—I guess it's all for nothing," he said, with a catch in his voice.

"Yeah, it's a real puzzle," Jake echoed. "Nothing to do now but wait for the redcoats to swarm us."

"Huh!" Reb snorted. "You'd complain if'n they hung you with a new rope."

There was a weary consensus from everyone.

Even Sarah appeared defeated. "It would take a real miracle to save us now." She moaned and slumped to the ground.

Suddenly Josh said angrily, "What did they bring us all here for if there was no hope? No one has told us the truth."

"No one, Josh?" Crusoe sat up a little straighter. "Not one person?"

"My own father lied to me. He said he'd be near me—'I'll be near you'—that's what he said. He lied to me!" The tears that he could not hold back ran freely down his face.

Josh knew that this had been in him for a long time —his bitterness at being forsaken in a strange world by his father. "He lied to me! He's not near me now and—"

"Isn't he, Josh?" Crusoe softly cut in.

Then Josh finally recognized it—something in Crusoe's voice tugged at the old memories buried deep in Josh's heart.

Josh stopped breathing and turned to look at the twisted form of Crusoe, at the piercing eyes that looked out from the old man's gnarled face.

"Isn't he near you, Josh? Right now?" Crusoe prodded.

Suddenly Josh knew! Why had he been so blind? he asked himself. He took a hesitant step toward Crusoe. His voice trembled as he spoke.

"Dad?"

Crusoe smiled, and Josh saw that beneath the beaten body it was indeed his father. Josh stumbled across the stone floor and fell into his father's frail grasp.

As the old man reached out and embraced his boy, there was much clearing of throats and looking off into the distance to avoid intruding on the moving reunion of father and son.

Finally Josh pulled away and wiped his face. "Why didn't I see?" he said. "Why didn't you tell me?"

"I didn't expect you to know me, Josh. The explosion changed me so much that not even your mother would have known me. She died in the explosion, son. And I didn't tell you because—well, I didn't know if you were strong enough to accept this." He gestured at his broken body and scarred face. "But now you can—and just in time."

Suddenly the pale face twisted with some hidden pain. Josh saw that the old man was paler than death.

"I—I think we have only a little time, Josh—"

"Dad, what's wrong!" Josh cried out and held the thin hand lightly, as if to keep his father from slipping off.

Suddenly Crusoe closed his eyes for a long moment as if he were listening to a distant call. Then he opened them, and a beautiful smile came to his lips. "It's time for me to go, Josh. I want you to know something. I'd always been proud of my boy, but now I'm proud of you as a man, for that's what you're becoming. Your mother would be proud of you too. Now be a strong man, Josh. Don't be afraid of anything. You will be guided by the wisdom of Goél—and he will keep you wherever you go."

Josh's father gave a little gasp at the end of the words, and then he squeezed his son's hand and smiled. "I'll see you in the morning, Josh."

The old man's eyes closed, and Josh knew that he was really alone on the earth.

17

Traitor Redeemed

Jake, how long are we going to have to stay in this place?"

The wiry redhead rolled over on his stomach and looked at Abbey, who was pouting a little.

"I dunno—but we better enjoy it while we can," he replied.

"Sure enough yes," Reb added. He pulled himself up from where he had been lying lazily on his back. He looked out into the distance. "I figure them priest fellers will be here soon enough."

"Well, I think somebody ought to do something!" Abbey said sharply.

Jake smiled. He and Reb both were drawn to Abbey's startling beauty, but they had quickly learned that she was spoiled to the bone. She seemed to take for granted that everyone would cater to her every whim.

Wash grinned at her and whispered to Jake, "I heard that Queen Victoria never looked to see if they was a chair behind her. Just sat down any time, like she figured it was somebody else's business to take care of those little details." He shook his head and then moved on.

Abbey seemed totally unaware of Wash's assessment. She was staring up at the highest point of the rim. There Josh and Sarah could be seen outlined against the sky, talking.

Then Jake spoke to Abbey, asking in a casual tone, "Well, who do you think ought to do something—and what?"

"Well, I'm not the one to say." Abbey hesitated. "But if Joshua would get his mind on the problem and stop spending so much time sulking around—" She suddenly paused, then smiled. "I mean, it is his responsibility, isn't it? Why doesn't he do something instead of wasting time?"

She looked up again at the couple on the high ground and shook her head. Then she glanced slyly at Reb, adding sweetly, "But I know that the rest of us could handle things quite nicely if Josh is just too busy."

With that, Abbey fell back into her own private thoughts.

* * *

Sitting on the ledge of the Needle, Sarah and Josh were unaware that the others were watching them.

"Josh, how many days has it been since we got here?"

Looking at the scratches he had made on the wall, Josh counted. "Nearly two weeks," he announced. "If we hadn't been able to snare those rabbits—and find those greens and onions—we'd have starved to death."

"Are we going to wait here much longer?"

"I don't know, Sarah. I guess after Dad died I was kind of shook up. But even now I don't know what we can do. I think I'm waiting for a miracle, and I don't even know what kind of miracle we need."

He tossed a stone over the edge, and they waited long moments before they heard it strike far below.

"Even if we left here and got away from Elmas and his crew, where would we go?" Josh wondered out loud.

"I don't know, Josh." Sarah drew a little closer. There was a loneliness and mystery in the vastness of the desert and the sky. "Everyone is getting restless—me too, I guess."

Suddenly Josh sat up and peered hard into the night, then let loose a long breath.

"Well, I guess we won't have to worry about what to do much longer. Look over there—see that light?"

"Way over there? Yes, I can barely see it. What is it?"

"I think it's the enemy. Two days ago, I sent the Hunters out to see how close the Sanhedrin were. I think the Hunters will be back by morning—with the bad news."

"Let's go inside, Josh. I'm getting cold."

They found the others sitting around a fire.

Josh broke the news at once. "I can see fires across the desert. I don't think it will be long now." Then he saw with surprise the Hunters sitting close to the fire, eating hungrily.

"Well, you must have snuck in the back way. Are they coming?" Josh asked Kybus.

"Maybe two days—maybe less."

"Josh, there ain't no way we can keep them fellers out of this roost," Reb complained. "It ain't a bad place to fight—if you got lots of help. But they's maybe ten paths that lead up here, and we can't watch all of 'em."

"Well, we'll just have to fight here—in this old building."

"But we'll be pinned down for sure," Jake said.

"We are anyway."

Josh looked around, then began to outline a plan. "Let's get all the food and water we have and move it in here. Volka, you start rolling the biggest rocks you can find into the openings. Just leave us enough room to shoot through. Some of you start clearing the stones and the bushes from around the building. Let's be sure they have to cross a wide open space to get at us."

"You believe it's going to do any good, Josh?" Wash asked.

"Nothing but a miracle will do any good now," Jake said.

167

"And miracles have been out of fashion for a few hundred years in Nuworld," Mat said grumpily.

"Ho, maybe we start them again." Tam grinned. "Come, we go clear the way."

One of the Gemini followed Josh. The other stuck close to Mat.

There was a great deal of activity the next two days —sharpening swords and arrows, storing food, moving stones. At dusk, no one was shocked when the Hunters announced that troops were coming up the passes.

"They're doing it smart too," Mat translated. "Using all the paths so we can't block them. Guess it was the best thing to move in here, Captain Josh."

Mat grinned at Josh almost cheerily.

Josh was amazed. "Well, Mat, if you start saying nice things, I guess a miracle can't be too far off."

Mat's face darkened. "Better not be. We're in trouble. I figure we can hold out maybe three or four days at most."

Late that night they got their first taste of the Sanhedrin. There was no warning—just a ball of fire that suddenly smashed against the side of the building and set the world aglow with blazing light.

"It's burning oil," Josh said. "Nothing we can do to put it out."

He dodged back as a small ball whizzed through one of the narrow ports. It fell on the floor and blazed up at once.

"They're fire bombs," Jake yelled. "Throw some of this dirt over the blaze."

They managed to put that one out with only a few singed fingers. Fortunately, the other bombs missed the ports and shattered on the outer walls.

"Can't see to shoot," Mat yelled. "That fire makes us blind as bats, and they can see us if we raise our heads."

"Everybody keep low," Reb warned. "We'll get 'em if they come through the winders—" He turned to Josh, and his eyes were alight with the joy of the battle. "Just like the Battle of Shiloh, ain't it, Josh?"

As Reb spoke, Josh saw a steel-helmeted guard dart through one of the side doors and launch a wicked spear straight at the young Southerner's back.

Wash with a yell threw his small body straight at Reb. The blow knocked Reb to the floor, and the spear passed harmlessly through the exact spot where he had been standing. Only Wash's quick action had saved his life.

Reb looked up to see Volka throw the soldier out. Then Volka rolled a large stone in front of the door.

Reb slowly got to his feet. He checked himself for injuries. Then he caught a glimpse of the spear embedded in the wall—the spear that would have killed him had it not been for Wash.

Reb looked at Wash who was now lying on the floor. He looked at the still black face steadily, then smiled. He put out his hand and said slowly, "Thankee, Wash."

Wash rose to his feet unaided and stared quizzically at Reb's outstretched hand.

But Reb didn't withdraw it. He continued to look at his friend for a long time and then said again, "Thankee, Wash."

Wash nodded and took Reb's hand. "Well, Reb, maybe in Goél's House everybody will be equal," he said.

And they turned to fight side by side.

It was a long night, for the troops of Elmas spared no trick to enter the besieged fortress. Their dead lay stacked like cordwood in the narrow openings.

Both sides had suffered heavy casualties. Sarah, nursing a spear cut in her left hand, was binding up Josh's thigh where he had suffered a sword wound. And the others were either getting medical attention or standing guard against the next attack.

Josh gazed at the wreckage of the room—bodies piled high at the entrances, blood over most of the floor, the defenders creeping painfully back to their posts.

Perhaps it was the utter hopelessness of their plight that made Josh suddenly grin and say to Sarah, "Wait till you hear my plan!"

She looked up at his smile, then said, "Well, let's hear it."

"When things get really bad we go to Phase Two."

"What's Phase Two?"

"When in danger or in doubt run in circles, scream, and shout!" he declaimed.

Then they both laughed as if they were back in Old-world.

"Josh, it's pretty futile, isn't it? I mean there's really no way out of this place, is there?"

Josh pulled the battered old black book out of his pocket and riffled the pages, then looked across at Sarah.

"We seem to be lost, Sarah, but the leaves of this old book are rustling with some wind. And I hear the wind say, 'It just isn't so.'"

"That sounds like something your dad might say."

"Probably is. You know, the odd thing is I'm not scared."

"Well, I'm not either. I think all the scare has been scared out of me."

"Maybe that's good. Maybe Goél has to get us to the brink of disaster before we listen to him."

"I think that's right, Josh, but—"

Sarah's words were cut short by a warning cry from Tam, who was watching one of the openings.

"Wake up! Somebody's coming!"

Now it was so quiet that Josh could hear what he thought was the sound of someone approaching the entrance. But this sound was different from footsteps. This was more like a slow scraping. Closer and closer it came.

Finally Tam whispered, "Get ready! They're here!"

Everyone stood poised with bows drawn and swords in hand.

The scraping noise grew louder. Then someone came slowly through the narrow opening, someone who was painfully crawling on bloody hands.

Josh watched with sword raised to strike. But as the figure crept into the dim light, he dropped his sword with a clatter and ran to the one who had collapsed on the floor.

"Dave!" Josh called.

The battered face of the missing Sleeper was touched with the silver moonlight.

"Is it really Dave?" Sarah cried. She fell down beside Josh, and they began to carry the still figure inside to a safer place.

Josh and Sarah placed Dave on a stone ledge, and Sarah held his head carefully. Dave was so still that Josh thought he was dead.

Suddenly, however, he opened his eyes and looked round at the battered little band. Then he smiled. "Well— I'm—I'm back," he whispered weakly.

"My land!" Reb breathed. "He looks like he's been sackin' wildcats and ran outta sacks!"

"Dave!" Josh cried out again. "How'd you get here?"

"They wanted me to—tell everything—about the Sleepers—and they made me—they made me—" His thin voice trailed off, and he turned his face to the wall.

Quickly, Josh reached out and took his hand. "Doesn't matter, Dave. You're back with us. That's all that counts."

"I'm so glad you're back, Dave!" Sarah said.

And then the other travelers began to gather close and spread warm little expressions of welcome and friendship.

As Dave turned his head to see them, his eyes glistened. "I've come," he whispered painfully, "I've come— to the House of Goél."

He pulled Josh down to whisper in his ear, but they all could hear his words. "Do you think that Goél—I mean, I know that I—I betrayed all of you, but do you think—he'll let me—in his House?"

"Sure! Sure he will, Dave!"

Immediately everyone chimed in with words of support.

Then Dave sat up and looked at them all. A smile lit up his broken features. It was as though a torch suddenly glowed brightly, then quickly faded, as his eyes closed. Now he had left them for good.

"He's gone, Josh," Sarah whispered.

"Not really," Josh answered as they laid him gently down. "Not really gone, Sarah."

In the middle of the silence, Mat said all of a sudden, "Well, there is our miracle—if we need it."

"Yes." Sarah shivered. "It's going to be easier to believe in Goél after this."

"If we could just get out of here!" Josh said. "I think we could really change this Nuworld some."

"But you can leave here—anytime you wish!"

The voice that suddenly rang out was familiar, but even Josh was suddenly struck dumb when a tall figure in a simple cloak stepped out of the shadows. There in the wan light of a port opening he saw Goél!

18

The River Road

He was the same as before, dressed in a gray cloak with nothing to announce his rank but his strong face. Those who were seeing Goél for the first time viewed him with awe. It was as though he embodied the assurance that people wait to experience all their lives. Goél spoke softly, but his words seemed to give safety. Everyone leaned forward a little as he spoke.

"I am Goél. That is one of my names. Later, you will learn others as we grow to know each other better."

He looked at them, and each would later swear that Goél looked at him alone. His gaze struck so deep that he seemed to see inside the most secret place of the heart.

"I have been building a House for many years, but today—with you—the House of Goél has its beginning in Nuworld."

"But—but . . ." Josh stammered. "We're nothing, Goél—just half grown!"

The strong face of Goél suddenly melted into a fine smile.

"I have chosen you, and I will strengthen you. All I ask is that you believe in me—all of you. Sleepers, Gemini, dwarfs, all people of Nuworld are invited, for you are my sheep from a strange fold. Now, who will follow Goél —to any danger?"

Without a single exception they all knelt at Goél's feet, and their lips and eyes expressed their love and willingness.

"Good! You will walk in dark places—but I will be there to be a light for you. You will never be alone. Now before I go, one word of counsel I will give." He smiled again and added, "It is written in the prophets that 'it is the honor of kings to search out a matter.' So, here is a thing for you to search out:

"Follow, follow the hidden way
    That flows down to the sea.
Pass on through the truth, my word obey,
    And come at last to me.

"Now I will leave you for a while."

"But, Goél," Josh said, scrambling to his feet. "What about—I mean all the old songs talk about seven Sleepers. We're only six now."

Goél looked at the boy searchingly and said, "Be of good cheer, Joshua, and never be afraid to ask too much of me. What do you want?"

A startling thought shot into Josh's mind. *But no, not even Goél can do that. On the other hand, it's worth a try.* Now, with Goél looking right into his eyes, almost as a dare, he blurted out what he was thinking.

"I—I want Dave to be one of us!"

Goél looked at Josh, and a broad and delighted smile lit up his strong face. He placed one hand on the boy's shoulder and said softly, "I have chosen well, my Joshua. You have great faith."

He turned and walked to Dave's body and touched the pale face lightly with his hand. He spoke softly at first. "David, you must return, for you are the servant of Goél."

Then Goél raised his voice to a shout that seemed to crack the rocks of the ancient structure. *"Return! Return! David! I command you!"*

174

Stunned by the sudden call, they all looked wildly at each other. Josh saw Dave's legs move, then his hands. Next his eyes opened, and he looked directly into Goél's face.

"You are now in the House of Goél, David!"

"Yes," Dave said strongly and sat up. "Yes, Goél."

Goél nodded. Then he turned and walked to Sarah. Gently he put his hands on her shoulders, and Josh saw her sway under their light pressure.

Very softly, but loudly enough for all to hear, Goél said, "Daughter, your road will be lonely. Those you trust most will betray you. That which you love best will be taken from you.

"But even when all is gone, if you will embrace the fate that waits for you, and if you will not rebel against it, a door will open before you. Behind that door you will find everything you have ever longed for."

He wheeled and looked deep into Reb's eyes. He was silent for a long moment. Then he spoke. "Your strength is your weakness, son. You will either learn to walk through deadly paths without a single weapon except your trust in Goél—or you will fail." Goél smiled and touched Reb's arm. "Throw your sword down, and let *me* be your strength."

Jake's lips were trembling as Goél stepped in front of him. The little redhead had never seemed afraid of anything, yet now he appeared deeply shaken past even fear.

"Son of Isaac," Goél said to Jake, "the seed of faith is in you. There will come a dark hour when every friend and every companion will abandon hope. In that hour of total and complete darkness, the fate of Nuworld will be in your hands. If *you* do not believe at that hour, there will be none who will believe, and all will be lost.

"And you, Wash, what will you do for Goél?"

175

The tall figure towered over the small youth. Yet in one way or another, when Wash looked up, he must have seen in Goél's strong face something that made him feel wanted. Tears in his eyes, Wash could only shake his head.

"You will be the key, my son, to unlock the hidden mystery. In the days ahead, when others are used and you seem to have no purpose in the House of Goél, remember what I say to you. The hour will come when you will offer the key that will unlock the mystery of all destiny."

"David," Goél said and simply looked at Dave, who had risen to his feet. "I will not force anyone to a task that he does not choose for himself. And the task I choose for you is the most difficult of any that I will give to the Seven Sleepers.

"I do not tell you what it is, but you must agree now—blindly—to accept what comes to you. It will be more difficult than you can ever imagine. Will you accept this quest?"

"Yes!" Dave said at once. "I will accept my part —whatever it is!"

"Do not forget," Goél bade him.

And then Goél turned once more to Josh. He put his hands on Josh's head, and Josh suddenly knelt. Goél leaned so close and spoke so softly that surely none but Josh himself could hear the words.

Suddenly his eyes opened, and he gasped, "But, Goél—" Then he looked up into the face of Goél and whispered, "Yes, I will do it."

Goél looked at all the Sleepers and finally turned to Abbey. He did not put his hands on her as he had with the others—not at first.

Abbey looked at him searchingly. Then she looked toward Josh and the others to find the support she suddenly needed. Finally she glanced up and said in a bare whisper, "Yes, Goél?"

He nodded with a slight smile in his warm eyes. "Daughter, you have been given much, perhaps too much. It is more difficult for those who have much. Tell me, daughter, would you give up the thing you prize most if I ask it of you?"

"Oh, yes, Goél!"

"What if I ask you for all your beauty?"

Abbey caught her breath. She had traded on her beauty for years. To lose it all—to be ugly! She probably could not conceive of such a fate, and her whole soul cried out against it. She could not speak.

"Well, what is your answer?" Goél pressed. He did not take his eyes from Abbey's face, and slowly she blushed a deep red of shame. Then her eyes fell.

"You cannot do that for me?" Goél asked quietly.

Abbey shook her head and began to sob. "Oh, I want to, but I just—can't!"

Goél looked down at the sobbing girl. Then he slipped his arm around her and lifted her up. He said gently, "I will take you where you are, Abbey, and not where I would like for you to be. But someday, I will ask you this again. When that day comes, I will have to have your final answer."

Suddenly he raised his hands over his head and cried, "All of you are now in my House. You are the servants of Goél! Even when you look for me and see me not, even then, believe. For I will be not only in the bright sunlight, but I will be in the darkness of the storm cloud. I welcome you, my friends, into the House of Goél!"

The ringing words were almost drowned out by a sudden rushing wind that swept through the ancient structure and seemed to rock the world. The columns swayed, and a flickering light touched every face.

Then the wind calmed, and the light faded to the old silver of the moon. In the stillness came one last whisper that Josh could never locate, except that later each would think it came from his own heart. "The House of Goél must be filled. Go into all the world."

A deep and total silence followed, washing through the old temple while they knelt in the moonlight.

"He's gone," Sarah whispered.

"Yes, but, you know, I can still feel him," Josh murmured. He looked at the others, trying to see if the difference he felt inside was visible to the eye. The room was the same. He could even hear faintly the activity of the Sanhedrin outside. But there was Dave, sitting quietly beside them as he had always been.

"Dave," Sarah whispered. "Are you all right?"

"Yes. For the first time in my life I'm all right." He touched Sarah's arm as if to reassure himself. Then he added, "It's good to be with you."

"Well," Mat said suddenly, "I have my reputation as a prophet of gloom to maintain, so I may as well point out that despite all that's happened, we're still in trouble." He waved his sword toward the door. "Won't be too long before we'll have company."

"Shoot, I reckon that's right." Reb nodded. "We can't go on forever! Even Stonewall knew when to back off and wait for another day!"

Dave shrugged and added, "I just can't believe that Goél would leave us here without something to go on."

Kybus suddenly quoted the last promise of Goél.

> "Follow, follow the hidden way,
> That flows down to the sea.
> Pass on through the truth, my word obey,
> And come, at last, to me."

Then he stopped, and they were all silent.

Josh wondered what the words meant.

Finally Jake said, "I wish he'd said just what he meant. I *hate* riddles!"

"Maybe he did," Josh said slowly.

"Did what?" Jake asked.

"Maybe he said exactly what he meant."

"But where's the *road*, Josh?"

Jake shook his red head in bewilderment. "What we need is a *real* road, with rocks on it you can pick up—not some sort of ideal way."

"Right." Wash nodded vigorously. "Like what we are standing in need of is a genuine, guaranteed, certified, literal road that will get us out of here."

"Listen," Mat said suddenly. "I think they're getting ready to make another rush. And they may have us this time. Get your weapons ready!"

"Wait," Josh said suddenly.

He held up his hand, and they all stopped their rush to the door as if they had run up against an invisible wall. "There's a time to fight, and there's a time to obey. And right now we're going to obey Goél."

"But *how*, Josh?" Sarah asked. "We don't know what—"

"We don't have time to do anything but obey Goél," Josh said. "Now listen. What do the words say? Never mind for now about what they mean. What do they say?"

"Well," Reb said slowly, his face twisted in thought, "the words say there's a road."

"Right," Josh cried. "Now, where is it?"

"Well, we don't really know," Jake said.

"Maybe we ain't supposed to know that," Reb suggested.

"Nonsense," Josh said. "The words tell us where the road is."

"Where, Josh?" Sarah asked in bewilderment.

"The words say, 'Pass on through truth.'"

"But, Josh—" Sarah shook her head with a smile. "That's just too vague. 'Truth'—why that could be anything."

"Let's take it literally," Josh said. He saw that none of them had the least idea of his meaning, so he pointed up at the wall and said, "Look!"

They all looked up, and there were the huge letters they had seen a hundred times:

YOU SHALL KNOW THE TRUTH
AND THE TRUTH
SHALL MAKE YOU FREE

They all stared blankly, then Sarah suddenly smiled a brilliant smile.

"Josh, you mean that 'truth' is right *there*."

"Can't see any other way," Josh said. "Let's look for some sort of a door or something right around that word *TRUTH*."

"But there's two of them," Jake said.

"We'll look at both." Josh straightened and looked at the doors. "Hurry! I think they're coming."

They all scurried to the wall and began to feel the apparently solid stone walls that were directly behind the word *TRUTH*. Almost at once Wash cried out, "I think I hit the jackpot!"

He pointed to a small steel lever that extended from between the cracks of stone. There was the outline of a massive door—a faint hairline crack, almost hidden by centuries of fine dust.

"Quick!" Josh urged. "They're coming!" He pushed

the lever. Silently the massive stone swung open to reveal a narrow tunnel that led down into the earth.

"Inside, right now!" Josh cried. He shoved them in like chickens, calling every name to make sure none was left. "Hunters, you first. It'll be dark inside, so you must guide us down. Volka, you next. Now you, Mat, Tam, and you, Amar and Rama—get in, now. Kybus, go along. Next, Sleepers—Dave, will you take Abbey's hand? Jake, now you. Reb, Wash, and Sarah—"

He touched them all lightly as they stepped inside, then Josh tripped the lever. Just as the massive gate began to close, he jumped inside to safety, only a second before the gate slammed in place with a conclusive thud.

"They'll never get through there!" he shouted as they began to walk downward. Even as they made their way along the passage, he thought he heard the faint, frustrated cries of the Sanhedrin, but then their babble faded to deadly silence.

Though it was completely dark, there was plenty of air. The Hunters led them carefully down the road that kept dropping more and more sharply. Finally, Josh was forced to lean backward to keep his balance. He could not judge the time, but it seemed a long while before the Hunters stopped and said something to Mat.

"They say that water is ahead," Mat relayed.

Sure enough, the little band had not gone too far before the sound of rushing water could be heard. Slowly they edged forward until finally they stood beside a stone wharf that bordered a small stream. Then one of the Hunters spoke again, and Mat translated.

"He says there are torches on the wall."

They groped around and discovered some dry sticks bound up and set in wall sockets. Soon they had made a fire and lit the torches. By the light, they saw five small wooden boats tied to the wharf.

"Who could have made those and left them here?" Dave wondered.

"I don't know, but they made them for us, I think," Josh said. "Everyone get in."

There was a scrambling and a few nervous cries from Abbey and the Geminis. Finally, with Volka on one craft all by himself, and the others comfortably settled, Josh addressed the company. "Volka, you go first, and Sarah and I will bring up the rear."

And so they slid away from the wharf, holding the torches high as they began their journey down the river.

"You know," Wash said, his voice echoing in the cavern, "I bet the crowd upstairs is beating their brains out, wondering what we've done with ourselves!"

They all laughed at the thought of the Sanhedrin trying to explain their failure to Elmas. Then they grew quiet and marveled at the beauty of the cave, where glittering diamond icicles hung from the ceiling. The stream channel was cool after the heat of the battle, and there was a silence that seemed to wrap them in a protective garment.

"Josh," Sarah said quietly after a long time, "we don't know where this river goes for sure, do we?"

"Sure we do, Sarah," Josh said with a broad grin. "Remember the last of the song? It said that the river 'leads, at last, to *me*.'"

He took a pull with the paddle and watched a silver fish swim under the boat.

After a little while he added, "I don't know how long this river is—and I don't know what lies around that next curve—but, Sarah, at the end of it we'll be sure to see one thing!"

"What's that, Joshua?" Sarah whispered.

Josh was sure she knew but wanted to hear him say it.

He caught up her hand and said in a glad voice, "At the end of this river we'll find Goél waiting for us!"

Other Titles from Moody Press and Gilbert Morris:

Kerrigan Kids #1

The Kerrigan Kids are headed to Africa to take pictures and write a story on a once fierce tribe. The Kids may be able to travel to Africa but if Duffy can't learn to swallow her pride and appreciate others, they may be left behind with their dreaded Aunt Minnie!
ISBN #0-8024-1578-4

Kerrigan Kids #2

With a whole countryful of places to explore and exciting new adventures to be had, the Kerrigan Kids can't help but have a good time in England. The Kerrigan Kids also learn an important lesson about having a good attitude and about being a good friend.
ISBN #0-8024-1579-2

Kerrigan Kids #3

After several mishaps including misdirected luggage, the Kerrigans are reminded that bad things can happen to good people and the importance of trusting in God even during difficult circumstances.
ISBN #0-8024-1580-6

Kerrigan Kids #4

The Sunday before they leave, the kids are reminded of the story of the Good Samaritan. When there is no one to meet their two new friends from the plane trip at the airport, the Kerrigan clan puts what they learned about helping other into practice.
ISBN #0-8024-1580-6

Bonnets and Bugles Series

Follow good friends Leah Carter and Jeff Majors as they experience danger, intrigue, compassion, and love in these civil war adventures (ages 10-14).

#1 Drummer Boy at Bull Run, 0-8024-0911-3
#2 Yankee Belles in Dixie, 0-8024-0912-1
#3 Secret of Richmond Manor, 0-8024-0913-X
#4 Soldier Boy's Discovery, 0-8024-0914-8
#5 Blockade Runner, 0-8024-0915-6
#6 Gallant Boys of Gettysburg, 0-8024-0916-4
#7 The Battle of Lookout Mountain, 0-8024-0917-2
#8 Encounter at Cold Harbor, 0-8024-0918-0
#9 Fire Over Atlanta, 0-8024-0919-9
#10 Bring the Boys Home, 0-8024-0920-2

The Seven Sleepers Series

For of old it was sung that the Seven Sleepers would awaken to unite their strength with Goel and join in battle against the wicked priests of the Sanhedrin. But the choice of Josh and each member of the quest is a dangerous one (ages 10-14).

#1 The Flight of the Eagles, 0-8024-3681-1
#2 The Gates of Neptune, 0-8024-3682-X
#3 The Sword of Camelot, 0-8024-3683-8
#4 The Caves That Time Forgot, 0-8024-3684-6
#5 Winged Raiders of the Desert, 0-8024-3685-4
#6 Empress of the Underworld, 0-8024-3686-2
#7 Voyage of the Dolphin, 0-8024-3687-0
#8 Attack of the Amazons, 0-80243691-9
#9 Escape with the Dream Maker, 0-8024-3692-7
#10 The Final Kingdom, 0-8024-3693-5

A Gilbert Morris Mystery

Join Juliet "Too Smart" Jones and her home-schooled friends as they attempt to solve exciting mysteries (ages 7-12).

#1 Too Smart Jones & the Pool Party, 0-8024-4025-8
#2 Too Smart Jones & the Buried Jewels, 0-8024-4026-6
#3 Too Smart Jones & the Disappearing Dogs, 0-8024-4027-4
#4 Too Smart Jones & the Dangerous Woman, 0-8024-4028-2
#5 Too Smart Jones & the Stranger in the Cave, 0-8024-4029-0
#6 Too Smart Jones & the Cat's Secret, 0-8024-4030-4
#7 Too Smart Jones & the Stolen Bicycle, 0-8024-4031-2
#8 Too Smart Jones & the Wilderness Mystery, 0-8024-4032-0
#9 Too Smart Jones & the Spooky Mansion, 0-8024-4029-0
#10 Too Smart Jones & the Mysterious Artist, 0-8024-4034-7

The Lost Chronicles

The Dark Lord has been busy, and once again Goel is sending the Seven Sleepers to spoil his plans. This time Josh and his friends are off to Whiteland, a place of sled dogs and igloos, polar bears and seals (ages 7-12).

#1 The Spell of the Crystal Chair, 0-8024-3667-6
#2 Savage Game of Lord Zarak, 0-8024-3668-4
#3 Strange Creatures of Dr. Korbo, 0-8024-3669-2
#4 City of Cyborgs, 0-8024-3670-6
#5 Temptations of Pleasure Island, 0-8024-3671-4
#6 Victims of Nimbo, 0-8024-3672-2
#7 Terrible Beast of Zor, 0-8024-3673-0